A
Broken
World

Cassidy Cornblatt

An Old Line Publishing Book

Printed in the United States of America

ISBN-13: 978-1-937004-54-5
ISBN-10: 1-937004-54-6

This book is a work of fiction. Any references to real people, events, establishments, organizations, or locales are intended solely to provide a sense of authenticity and are used fictitiously. All other characters, incidents, and dialogue are drawn from the author's imagination and are not to be construed as real.

Cover Design by Christopher Saghy

Old Line Publishing, LLC
P.O. Box 624
Hampstead, MD 21074
Toll-Free Phone: 1-877-866-8820
Toll-Free Fax: 1-877-778-3756
Website: www.oldlinepublishingllc.com

To my brother Ryley,
for always believing in my story and for helping me share
that story with the world.

Chapter 1

Caleth was shaken awake from a troubled sleep. He painstakingly lifted his heavy eyelids to see his mother standing over him. He groaned as he came to realize that the sun had not yet risen, but he knew that this was how his life would be for the next four years. The season had changed to the falling of leaves, and with it came the time when youths who had recently turned sixteen departed for the battle school.

"Come on, Caleth," his mother spoke pleadingly, "you have to get up. Don't make this any more difficult than it already is."

"I'm coming, Mom," Caleth replied. "This will just take some getting used to, that's all."

"I know, but you'll be fine. Don't worry about it."

With great effort, Caleth hoisted himself out of the bed and got dressed. Then he ate a hurried breakfast and bid farewell to his family. It would be a long time before he would see them again. He tried not to think about that as he rushed out the door and instead tried to concentrate on what lay ahead.

◊◊◊◊◊◊◊

There were at least thirty kids at the meeting spot, and these were only the sixteen-year-olds from an area encompassing four villages. There were many such areas in Jokatone that sent children to the battle school. This was to be expected since the kingdoms of Jokatone and Quantoff had been at war for the past hundred years. After four mandatory years of training, graduates were sent off to serve Jokatone in the field of battle. Only after these eight years of service could people settle down and create a life for themselves.

Caleth checked in with the representative from the battle school and then hung to the edge of the group. Some people were talking to others they knew, but Caleth wasn't in the mood for talking. He didn't even know a large portion of the people there. He may have seen them briefly on market days or at other such times, but he had never really conversed with them. It was also a little intimidating since most people, unlike him, were carrying weapons their parents had given them. Caleth's parents used no weapons. They were both spellcasters who had used their art in defense of their kingdom and now used their skills to help people in the surrounding villages.

As the group began the walk to the battle school, Caleth contemplated his fate. He knew that the battle school separated its pupils into two groups: those who used weapons and those who used spells. He assumed that he would be put into the spellcasting group since both his parents had been, but there was always the chance he would be forced to wield some type of weapon, especially since almost three-fourths of the people who attended became fighters. Unfortunately, no one knew beforehand whether they could cast spells because their inner spirit had to be Awakened, which took a secret spell that few knew. When people tried to replicate it using what they observed when it was cast upon them, it often ended in death for both the caster and those he was casting it upon. Needless to say, few people tried, and the young just had to wait to be categorized for their future.

As they approached the battle school, Caleth saw his new home for the first time. He had never been this far from his village, and the school didn't look very inviting. It was more like an otherworldly fortress than a place of learning, defensible from every angle and even surrounded by a moat filled with lava. A massive bridge spanned the moat and did not seem to be affected by the molten rock below it. In fact, as he walked across it, he touched the side and was surprised to find it cool. There was no way Caleth could see to bring the bridge up, but he figured there must be some way to do it, because the school seemed to be perfectly defensible in every other conceivable way. The battle school was the most impressive thing Caleth had ever seen, and it didn't seem possible that he would be spending the next four years of his life living inside it.

Upon entering the battle school, the group was led to a large chamber where an old man stood waiting in the center of the room. He was surrounded by many chairs all facing toward him. Next to each chair was a small, empty, glass cylinder that seemed to be very important. The man who led the group to the battle school told the children to take a seat and obey the old man, whom he referred to as Master Judge Maquias. After everyone had sat down in a chair, Master Maquias spoke.

"Here you will be separated into those with magical aptitude, and those with none," he stated. "Close your eyes, place your hand on top of the cylinder next to your chair, and concentrate on what I say. Feel your inner self Awaken. *Awanin seyon.* Experience your mind becoming one for the first time. *Kinowan ji seyon oniquon.*

Listen to yourself as you never could before. *Ka horandir da kinowan ji seyon.*"

At first, Caleth had no idea what Master Maquias was saying. He hadn't felt different. However, now he could sense another presence within his mind that, though less familiar, was just as natural as his regular conscience. Unfortunately though, his mind was not merging with this new presence. His inner spirit was taking control of his mind.

"Do not fight with your inner spirit," Master Maquias continued. "*Nakan ka jikona di seyon.* Only time can bind it with your mind. *Yewol dingra kinowan ji seyon.* Create something by drawing on the powers of your joined mind. *Ka wazak grefa di kinowan ji seyon.*"

Caleth attempted to relax as his inner spirit took over and drew power in a great surge from his mind. For one moment, he was filled with excruciating pain, and the next, he was more exhausted than he had ever been before.

"Open your eyes," commanded Master Maquias. "If your cylinder is empty, you must leave the room and become a fighter."

The group all obeyed, and looking around the room, they were astonished by what they saw. Although most of the glass cylinders remained empty, there were several that now contained things. Caleth looked in amazement at the cylinder next to his chair. There was a small sphere hovering inside. It appeared to consist of an ice cold core, covered with a coating of flames and enveloped with dancing lightning. Strangest of all, it seemed to be pulsing with a life of its own.

Caleth glanced around at some of the other filled cylinders. In one next to a girl from his village, snow was falling. In another, lightning was continually striking, and in a third, a pool of slime bubbled at the bottom. Before he could finish his survey of the room, a smashing sound brought his attention back to his own cylinder. The sphere seemed to have gained an awareness of its situation and was now hurling itself against the sides of its enclosure.

"Umm, could I have a little help here?" Caleth inquired.

Master Judge Maquias hurriedly hobbled over.

"What seems to be the problem?" he asked.

Caleth gestured towards his cylinder. Master Maquias frowned for a moment, and then spoke.

"You seem to have created a quazicar," he stated. "That is a living creature that is rarely seen by men. They typically live in regions far away from our towns and villages. Although you cannot see it with the naked eye, these creatures do have eyes and mouths and such. However, they prefer to communicate telepathically with others of their kind. Quazicars are made up of ice, fire, and lightning, and they can use each of these as weapons against their enemies. This quazicar cannot live in the vacuum of the glass cylinder. It must escape or it will die."

As Master Maquias was speaking, the quazicar had been freezing the glass, and now a ring of fire exploded from it into the sides of its container, causing the glass to shatter with the rapid change in temperature.

"Don't touch it!" Master Maquias shouted. "If the quazicar is angry, it could severely injure anyone it touches!"

However, the quazicar did not seem to care about the other people in the room. It just flew up next to Caleth's head and hovered there. Upon seeing that the quazicar did not attack, Master Maquias told Caleth to keep it since it seemed to like him, although in truth he was just afraid to take it away because he was sure that that would result in injury, and he was already tired from releasing the inner spirits of the children. After this situation was taken care

11

of, Master Maquias spoke to those children who remained in the room.

"Congratulations," he said, "you have all just become new members of the spellcasting division of the battle school. Over the next four years, you will develop your magical potential and choose your specialization. This first magical experience often symbolizes the specialization that a wizard will choose. For example, many people who summon frost choose to specialize in ice magic or water magic. I hope you will choose wisely because knowledge is the key to unlocking the world, and your specialization will determine which part of the world you will master."

Caleth knew about specializations. His mother specialized in lightning and his father in healing. Caleth's father was the best healer in his village and even the best in the surrounding villages, and Caleth's mother had once started a man's heart using a quick jolt of electricity after the man's heart had stopped suddenly during a healing spell Caleth's father was casting. However, Caleth didn't know what his first spellcasting experience said about his specialization. Maybe he would specialize in summoning, or using the elements, but he hoped he could specialize in something more like merging all types of spellcasting into a single form.

"After you leave this room," Master Maquias continued, "you will follow the man standing outside of the door. His name is Logart, and he will take you to your new rooms. There you will find robes fit for students of your status, and an individualized schedule will be delivered to each of you tomorrow morning after breakfast. Spend the time until then getting to know your roommates and future companions. I bid you all good luck in your future endeavors."

Chapter 2

Breakfast the next morning was at six-o-clock sharp. All of the new students were bleary-eyed from lack of sleep and could hardly believe this would be their life for the next four years. Caleth looked around the great hall at all of the battle school spellcaster pupils. The older students were all sitting with friends from previous classes, but all of the beginner students were seated at the far side of the hall, closest to the doors. There were at least a hundred of them.

The quazicar was still hovering beside Caleth, who had named it Quazi. As Caleth ate, Quazi did too. At least, it seemed that way since Quazi would zip down to the plate, and the next moment a fruit chunk would be gone.

The day before, the elder pupils had showed the newcomers around the school and then had left the beginning students to get to know one another. Caleth had hung back from the crowd, and hadn't talked to anyone. He had been too wiped out from his spellcasting experience to have enough energy left to converse. Now he was paying the price, though, as he sat alone with only Quazi for company. It didn't help that he was the only one with a small spherical creature hanging around his head.

After breakfast, the battle school pupils headed back up the stairs to their rooms, and when they got there, they found a schedule lying on each of their beds. Caleth's schedule was as follows:

- Breakfast: 6:00am to 7:00am
- Basic Spellcasting/Controlling the Inner Spirit – (Group A): 7:30am to 9:30am
- Beginning History: 10:00am to 12:00pm
- Lunch: 12:00pm to 1:00pm
- The Art of Blending Magics: 1:30pm to 3:30pm
- Spellcasting Accompaniments – (Group C): 4:00pm to 6:00pm
- Dinner: 6:00pm to 7:00pm
- Free Time: 7:00pm onwards

Caleth compared his schedule with other people in the room. Most people had Basic Spellcasting, Beginning History, and Spellcasting Accompaniments at the same time, but in different groups. The third class appeared to be a specialized class. Caleth couldn't find anyone in the same class as him for that period. There appeared to be five groups for Basic Spellcasting and Spellcasting Accompaniments: A through E. If there were around one hundred beginner students, this would make the class size around twenty people.

A few minutes later, elder spellcasters came to take the students to their new classes. Caleth gathered with the Group A people and followed the group down to the room where their class was being held. The room consisted of rows of desks that each had three glasses of water lined up on top of them. The teacher was a balding man with a permanent scowl who seemed to be thinking that beginning spellcasters were always trouble.

The students took their seats and class began. The teacher, Professor Wazquat, started by calling role and then began a lecture on the safe and controlled use of magic. After an hour and a half, he told the students to freeze the water in their glasses using the magic word 'ikanjau'. He told them it was necessary to grasp the glass in one hand while casting the spell in order to focus it on a specific area. Otherwise, the whole room might accidently be lowered to a freezing temperature. When they had accomplished this task, they were to see him.

Caleth thought it was odd that if each person had a specialization, they could also cast spells from other spheres of magic. Perhaps they were only specialized after they left the battle school because they were almost solely taught their specialization in later years. For now though, Caleth pushed this to the back of his mind and concentrated on the spellcasting exercise.

As the Professor had instructed, Caleth took hold of one of the glasses on his desk and spoke, "*Ikanjau.*" He felt his inner spirit doing something, as if it was giving out power, and Quazi swelled to twice his normal size. As Caleth was busy staring at the now bloated quazicar, he felt his hand grow cold. Turning back to look at the glass of water, he saw that it had been completely turned to ice. He called over Professor Wazquat and showed him the glass and the engorged quazicar, which was shrinking back to its normal size even as he spoke. Professor Wazquat was silent for a moment, still with his ever present scowl, and then he spoke to Caleth.

"It seems to me that your little creature has done your work for you," he sneered. "I would guess that upon hearing the magic word to freeze the water, it wanted to help you, so it drew upon your power and did the work itself. You need to put the creature away, so you can learn yourself."

"But," Caleth replied, "I don't know how to stop him."

"Have you tried stuffing the little thing into your pocket? That ought to do the trick."

"Uh, no, but wouldn't it hurt to touch him."

"That's your problem, not mine," the Professor stated as he walked away.

So Caleth braced himself as he reached out to Quazi, and was surprised to find that it didn't hurt to touch him. He carefully placed Quazi into the pocket in his robe with a little murmur of, "I'll let you out as soon as I can." Quazi didn't seem to mind; he quickly settled into a comfortable position and seemed to fall asleep. With that, Caleth turned his attention back to the two other glasses of water sitting on his desk.

"*Ikanjau,*" he said as he grasped the glass of water with one hand. This time, nothing happened. He tried concentrating harder. "*Ikanjau,*" he spoke again, but only managed to get the surface to freeze. Thus passed a frustrating thirty minutes in which Caleth only managed to get the water to freeze once, and then in his excitement to tell the Professor, had accidently knocked the glass onto the floor, where it promptly shattered, destroying the evidence of his accomplishment.

The other beginning students were faring just as badly. Only one or two actually managed to complete the task, and that was in the last couple minutes of class. The rest suffered miserably through their failures, confident that this was how it would be for the rest of their lives. One person even managed to freeze his hand onto his glass and to remove it, had Professor Wazquat cast a spell to warm the glass.

As soon as the class let out, Caleth took Quazi out of his

pocket. Excited to be free once again, Quazi flew rapidly around in the air above Caleth until finally settling down into his usual spot to the left of Caleth's head. Caleth chuckled at Quazi's antics as he walked back to the common room.

After he arrived, he found the Beginning History group and waited for the rest of the people to get there. Once everyone was accounted for, they were all taken down to an enormous lecture hall. The teacher there was a young woman called Professor Lithwa. She was extremely excited about her subject and was nearly jumping for joy as she told the class how the first wizard had his inner spirit Awakened by a golden dragon and how this man was taught the Spell of Awakening to use for the good of his people. It was interesting, but not exactly something Caleth thought would be useful in the days ahead.

◊◊◊◊◊◊◊

After an uninteresting lunch, Caleth was taken to The Art of Blending Magics. He was the only beginning student attending this class, and although it was kind of daunting, it was also exciting.

Caleth sat down next to a tired-looking boy who was probably in his second year. The teacher, an old man with a full gray beard, must have been of higher status than Caleth's other teachers, because he had the title of Master Spellblender Trifus. Master Trifus started out his class with a lesson on the difficulty of combining magics. Each student was to create an ant consisting entirely of electricity, but still alive.

Caleth wasn't comfortable with using magic on his own yet, so he kept Quazi out for this lesson. Unfortunately, though, he did not know the magic words to create an electric ant. He turned to the boy next to him.

"What do I say to create an ant out of electricity?" he asked.

The boy laughed in his face. "How do you not know the words?" he replied. "What are you, a first year?"

"Actually," said Caleth, "yes."

"What?! How is that possible?! I didn't think first years were allowed in this class."

"I don't know. Maybe it was because of my first spellcasting experience. I created this." He gestured towards Quazi.

"Wow," the boy replied as his facial expression changed to one more like awe, "you must be pretty powerful. I guess I'll help you out then, but can you even cast spells yet?"

"Not completely, no. But my quazicar can. I'm sure it won't change the experience."

"Okay," said the boy, "you'll need to use the word 'miniquo' for ant, 'fachalan' for lightning, and 'konhekto' for summon. By the way, my name's Ganlo if you need anything else."

"Thanks, Ganlo," Caleth stated, as he turned back to his desk on which a glass cage was waiting. "Let's see how this goes," he mumbled to himself as he held the cage. "*Konhekto fachalan miniquo,*" he said. Quazi swelled to twice his size, and an ant appeared in Caleth's cage. It was just a regular ant, and a second after it appeared, it was struck down by lightning. "Hmm," Caleth mumbled. As soon as Quazi had shrunk back to his normal size, Caleth tried again. "*Konhekto miniquo fachalan.*" Quazi expanded again. This time many ants fell from the top of the cage in the shape of a lightning bolt. "Not quite right either," Caleth thought. He turned to Ganlo.

"What word means 'from'?" Caleth inquired.

Ganlo looked up from his own cage, in which there was an ant made of lightning, but it wasn't living. "'Di' is the word we use for common prepositions," he replied. "It actually means with, but it typically works."

Caleth turned back to his cage for another attempt. This time he said, *"Konhekto miniquo di fachalan."* Quazi grew larger, and as Caleth watched his cage, an ant with electricity zapping across its body appeared. As Caleth stared at this creation, the ant began to move. It slowly started crawling around its enclosure. With an excited smile on his face, Caleth showed Ganlo.

"Whoa," Ganlo said, "how were you able to do it?"

"I just said the right combination of words, and my quazicar did the rest."

"That's so cool. I wish I had one of those."

Any further conversing was abruptly cut off as Master Spellblender Trifus started into a lecture on the complexity of combining multiple magics. Caleth listened with a smile on his face. For the first time that day, things were finally looking up.

◊◊◊◊◊◊◊

Spellcasting Accompaniments was an interesting class, and probably the most useful out of those Caleth was taking. Of course, it didn't hurt his review of the class to have a beautiful girl named Flioba sitting next to him and constantly asking him for help. This class was taught by a large man called Professor Brocton. It was meant to teach the students some of the words, gestures, drawings, writings, and objects that went along with spellcasting.

One of the first things they did in this class was to learn some of the gestures that could be used when casting spells. For example, when targeting a specific object as the subject for a spell, the arm would curl out from the body in an arc to point at the target. A spell with a burst effect would be used with a gesture similar to when targeting an object except instead of pointing with a finger, a clenched fist would be extended that would be unclenched when the arm was straight. A spell cast on oneself would be used with a gesture of swirling a hand around the person's head.

After learning the use of gestures, the group was given the same task as in Basic Spellcasting, except this time they had gestures to help them as well. Caleth thought he could do it this time. Instead of just holding the glass in one hand, Caleth decided to unclench his hand as he said the magic word to stimulate the freezing effect to start in the center of the water and spread to the edges. Surprisingly, this worked on the first try. Pleased with his success, Caleth showed Flioba, who was trying to use the target burst gesture and was only succeeding in chilling the room.

◊◊◊◊◊◊◊

That night at dinner, Caleth began his meal alone, but after a few minutes, he was joined by Ganlo. It seemed he finally wasn't an outcast.

During his free time, Caleth practiced casting spells without help. He resolved to go through the next day without Quazi's assistance. Things were going well for him.

Chapter 3

The next few months passed without incident. Caleth learned how to cast spells without Quazi and was excelling in all his classes. He had become good friends with Ganlo and was working on becoming chummy with Flioba. He had also figured out that nearly any spell would go the way he wanted if he just found the right way to order the words and used specific spell accompaniments.

On one particular day in winter, Caleth was listening to a lecture in The Art of Blending Magics on how to create a portal that connected worlds or parts of worlds. It involved conjuration to make the portal and lightning to bridge the gap between the two places. Master Spellblender Trifus was going to allow the students to make an attempt at this blend of magics after he first showed them a demonstration.

"Now when you are going to try this," he said, "you will only be making a portal to the rainforest to summon a frog. While conjuring the portal, you will be using the word 'groufel' to refer to the rainforest, and 'bunac' to refer to the frog. On the other hand, I thought I would cast something a little more interesting. I will be creating a portal to the Plane of Elementals, and I will summon a nikian, which is a small, rabbit-like, earth elemental. For this demonstration, I will not be drawing a warding circle to contain the creature I am summoning, but whenever you summon anything even slightly dangerous, you should always draw a warding circle for protection. Are there any questions before I begin?"

Someone in the back raised his hand.

"Yes, Jarn?"

"I was wondering why someone would conjure a portal to summon something," said Jarn, "when they could just summon it directly."

"That's a good question, Jarn. Well, can a person summon himself to somewhere else?"

"Uh, no; At least, I don't think so."

"No he cannot. So in order to transport yourself, you must conjure a portal. Portals are also used to allow multitudes of people to quickly travel lengthy distances. However, portals can be seen, and anyone, or anything, can go through one, so you should always be careful when dealing with them. Does that answer your question?"

"Yes, sir."

"Now I will proceed with the demonstration," stated Master Trifus. "Watch how I move my arms when I cast this spell. The size of the portal depends on the size of the ellipse I make with them." Master Trifus held both arms above his head as high as he could stretch them and laid one of his hands over the other. Then he slowly lowered his arms in a large ellipse as he uttered, "*Wazak huelnef da Kalamo ji agrakar di fachalan.*" His hands touched at the base of the ellipse, and the spell was closed. Sparks flickered on the outline of the ellipse as a dark mass slowly expanded outward to fill the interior. As the dark material touched the sparks, they streaked inwards towards the center, and with a loud bang and a sharp crackle, they disappeared into the void.

"As you can see," Master Trifus stated as he turned to face the class, "the portal part of the spell is complete. Next I will summon the nikian." He turned back towards the portal. "I am going to place a lit candle on this side of the portal to hasten the summoning. Creatures are more inclined to enter the portal when there is something to guide them through to the other side."

He lit a small candle and placed it on the ground in front of the portal, then he held his right arm out towards the portal and made his hand into a circle. He slowly put his index and middle fingers of his left hand through the circle of his other hand and bent them into a hook-like shape hanging on the part of the circle made by his thumb. As he was making this gesture, he uttered, *"Konhekto nikeana di huelnef."*

Nothing happened at first, but a few seconds later, a small, earthy-looking head emerged from the portal, followed by the body. The nikian looked like a rabbit made from the earth itself, and being an earth elemental it was made of what looked like clumps of dirt with moss growing all around the body in place of fur. Where the bushy tail should have been, a shrub with silky-looking leaves was growing.

Master Trifus picked up the nikian and showed it to the class. It did not struggle as he held it and acted like a docile, pet rabbit. After the class was done observing it, he put the nikian down and gave it a little push towards the portal. The nikian hopped contentedly back through to its home plane.

Master Trifus turned back towards the class with a smug smile at his own power and began to give a small lesson on the nature of the Plane of Elementals. He never saw the large, fiery head that looked out through the portal behind him until it was already too late.

"Look out!" someone shouted from the back of the classroom as the head disappeared back through the portal and a huge blazing arm reached through and latched onto Master Trifus, who promptly fainted.

Caleth acted without thinking. He quickly let Quazi out of his pocket and reached his arm out towards the portal. While he had been at the battle school, he had learned many things, including how to reverse a spell. He opened his mouth and the words came to him, although from where he did not know.   Caleth chanted, *"Kazaw huelnef ji kweltow fachalan di quentiv."* Then he clenched his fist as Quazi expanded to an enormous size and with a sudden, screeching sound the portal snapped shut, severing the arm of the creature that was holding Master Trifus.

The flames racing across the arm jumped to twice their normal size as the arm fell to the ground, but strangely they did not seem to burn the floor. The arm started to shake and then with a burst of light, it was gone leaving only a pile of ashes and a large red gem where it had been. Caleth fell to the ground and felt blackness come across his consciousness.

◊◊◊◊◊◊◊

Caleth woke up in a hospital bed aching all over and barely able to sit upright. As he gazed about his surroundings, he noticed that Master Trifus was sitting by his bed.

"Sir," Caleth said, "what are you doing here?"

"You saved my life," Master Trifus answered, "and I thought seeing how you were doing was the least I could do, not that you need me to look after you while you've got your quazicar." Caleth looked behind him and saw Quazi hovering by his bedside.

"Thank you, sir. But what was the creature that attacked you?"

"It was a galakanth, a vicious hunter on the Plane of Elementals. It seems the galakanth was in pursuit of the nikian before its prey escaped through the portal. When the nikian went back, it must have managed to sneak by the galakanth without being spotted because the galakanth decided to go into the portal to go after its prey. When it saw me instead, it thought I would make an even better meal, so it attacked. You shut the portal before it had time to pull me through."

"I don't even know how I shut it."

"Well, you have real talent, Caleth. It would be a shame to waste it. Here, I want you to have this." He held out an amulet consisting of a gold chain and the red gem that was left from the galakanth arm. "It's an eternal fire gem. It is supposed to bring love and warmth to you when you need it most. It also enhances your fire magic."

Caleth slipped the amulet over his neck. "Thank you, sir. I will keep it with me at all times."

"Good, it could be very useful. Anyway, I have to get back to my room to prepare for my next lesson. You should be able to get back to your classes tomorrow. You passed out under the strain of the powerful spell you cast, and sleep should allow you to recuperate. Oh, and the Head Caster of the school wants to meet with you after this semester is over. I think he has an assignment for you."

Chapter 4

The three weeks until the end of the semester seemed to have raced by afterwards, although each day felt drawn out and slow. Final exams passed by smoothly. Caleth thought they were easy, though not everyone would agree. As long as he knew the right words, he could pretty much arrange his words and gestures to cast anything, although an occasional mishap did occur and some spells took longer to get right than others.

The hardest test for Caleth was history because it involved the memorization of events and not spells, but even this was relatively simple because the class didn't go into much detail, only laying the framework for other history classes in the future.

The day after the semester ended, as the students relaxed in their common room after breakfast, some of the elder spellcasters began to pass out schedules for the winter semester. When they got to Caleth, they didn't give him a schedule like the rest. They gave him a small piece of paper with the words: "See Head Caster

Glantius." When Caleth first received this, he was worried that he had done something wrong, but he soon remembered that Master Trifus had said he would be given an assignment by the Head Caster.

After he realized why he had been called to the Head Caster, Caleth became curious as to what his assignment would be. He searched around for one of the elder spellcasters and asked them where to find the Head Caster. Apparently it was a stupid question because "everyone knows the Head Caster resides in the room at the top of the central spire at the battle school," or at least that's what one of the elder spellcasters said. Feeling slightly annoyed at being insulted, Caleth left the common room.

Reaching the spire was less complicated than Caleth had expected. Once outside, it was easily visible above the surrounding buildings and getting to it was simple. Inside, a continually-revolving, spiral staircase took people to the different areas off the inner column. Caleth rode the staircase all the way to the top and then got off onto a small, stone platform leading to a wooden door. He timidly approached the door and knocked softly.

"Come in," a voice spoke from within.

Caleth opened the door and entered the chambers of the Head Caster. The room he entered was lavishly decorated and contained a desk and three chairs along with many ornamental items. Two people were seated in the room. In one chair sat an old man with a long, gray beard and sagging features. Permanent scowl lines marked his face and hinted at his short temper with those who did not follow his orders to the letter. Caleth was disturbed by this appearance, since he had hoped the Head Caster would be a wise and kind man. Much to Caleth's surprise, seated in another chair was Flioba, who looked as worried as he about what the Head Caster had to say.

"Take a seat," commanded the Head Caster. Once Caleth was seated, the Head Caster began. "This school consists of classes and assignments," Head Caster Glantius spoke. "You both have made remarkable progress in your respective classes, you, Caleth, with your victory over the galakanth, and you, Flioba, with your mastery of the Ice Dome spell, a most difficult spell indeed."

Caleth looked down at his feet in embarrassment as his accomplishment was mentioned and Flioba blushed at her own.

"Do not be embarrassed by your successes," the Head Caster continued. "You should be proud of what you have achieved. Due to your accomplishments, I have decided to give you both an assignment that you should be able to handle." He paused for effect. "I want you two to infiltrate a Quantoff battle camp and bring me information about their next plan of attack. I will be sending an experienced fighter with you to serve as a guard in case of trouble. Make sure you are not noticed."

"How are we to get into their camp?" Caleth asked.

"That is up to you," the Head Caster replied. "I have no patience for those who cannot think for themselves. Just make sure to do as I have told you. You will pay the price for any mistake you make. The fighter will meet you right outside the school. He will have any supplies you might need. You may go now." Head Caster Glantius gestured dismissively, indicating that this was a command and they should not linger.

◊◊◊◊◊◊◊

Caleth and Flioba left the Head Caster's chambers in silence, both contemplating their journey ahead. Caleth felt a thrill of adventure and was excited to begin this assignment, whereas Flioba thought she would rather stay at the battle school with her new friends than travel off with two boys she hardly knew. Both worried about their ability to complete the assignment. Finally, Caleth broke the silence.

"What is the Ice Dome spell?" he asked.

"Just a bubble-like shield made of ice that can be projected onto people or objects away from oneself," Flioba answered, modest about the full scope of the spell and the strain it took to cast.

"I assume ice spells are your specialty then?"

"Yes, what's yours?"

"Spell blending."

"Oh, that sounds cool. What's a galakanth, and how did you defeat it?"

"It's a fire elemental from the Plane of Elementals. All I did was close the portal from which it was emerging." Caleth blushed modestly.

Caught up in their conversation, they arrived at the bridge that spanned the moat of lava. They both took a deep breath and then crossed through the gateway to the outside world. An adventure awaited them, and an assignment hungered to be fulfilled.

Chapter 5

A short, young man with a scraggly beard met Caleth and Flioba at the end of the bridge. He had a gaunt face and hollow cheeks with a maniacal grin plastered on his face. He wore chainmail armor beneath his travel clothes and had a war hammer strapped to his back. With him were three horses, each carrying supplies and ready to ride.

"Me an' Fred have been waitin' fer ya fer quite some time," he spoke. "What took ya so long?"

"We had to speak with the Head Caster," Caleth replied. "I assume you know our assignment."

"Oh aye," stated the man.

"Who's Fred?" interjected Flioba.

"Me war hammer," answered the man. "Used t' belong t' my grandmammy, quite a fearsome gal she was. I take good care of it fer her, just like she wanted me to."

"What's your name?" asked Caleth, who was beginning to feel

a bit frightened of their guard.

"Grippard," stated the man. "Don't know what help I'll be in thinkin', but I'm pretty good at my specialty."

"What's that?" Flioba asked.

"Skull crushin'!"

"Great," thought Caleth, "now we have a slightly crazy man who's good at crushing skulls protecting us." This adventure wasn't looking like so much fun to him now.

Before the conversation could delve deeper into the current grisly topic, Caleth interrupted. "We should probably head out," he said. "I don't think the Head Caster would approve of our loitering about."

Since all young children in Jokatone were taught at a young age how to ride their journey began smoothly and almost effortlessly. The only thought to darken their bright start was the question of how to get into the battle camp in the first place. Caleth wanted more information.

"So what do you know about this camp?" he asked Grippard.

"I know it's a good-size camp an' used most of'en fer raidin'," Grippard responded. Most o' the warriors they gotst are new recruits, but they do gotst a couple o' higher rankin' officers."

"How does Quantoff recruit its fighters?" Caleth inquired. An idea was forming in his mind.

"Me an' Fred 'ave heard they send warriors out t' the villages t' round up all able-bodied men an' women." Nowadays, women fought alongside men in battle, but Caleth had once heard that this hadn't always been the case. "Then the selected people are t' report t' a camp fer trainin'," Grippard continued.

"Maybe we could get into the camp posing as new recruits," Caleth thought aloud.

"That'll never work," replied Grippard. "They keep a book

where they be puttin' all o' the names o' the recruits. If youse not in that book, they kill ya. Expectin' spies I would guess, which is kin' o' what we are anyways."

Caleth and Flioba exchanged a smile. "We'll get into the camp," Caleth stated. "We can write our names in the book using a distance spell to control the quill. That kind of magic is easy stuff."

With their method of entry into the battle camp decided, they continued on light-heartedly, never fearing there might be trouble before they reached their destination.

◊◊◊◊◊◊◊

The next two days passed uneventfully as Caleth, Flioba, and Grippard rode from dawn until dusk, and then set up camp for the night. On the third day, it began to rain, dampening their spirits and slowing their progress. Luckily, Grippard had packed extra clothing so they would not have to sleep in their damp clothes, which would have been very uncomfortable. Midway through the fourth day, the clouds loomed dark and menacing overhead, pouring torrents of cold rain down upon them. They reached the end of Jokatone's borders, marked by a short, stone wall and a welcome sign that had long since fallen off its post and laid rotting beneath.

"We 'ave just entered the Desolate Fields," Grippard informed them. "This land between our border an' Quantoff's is unclaimed, an' fer good reason. This is where most o' the battles take place." He gestured towards the broken shaft of a spear sticking out of the ground a short distance away for emphasis.

"Have you ever been in a battle?" Flioba asked.

"Fred's crushed many foes, but myself, I've only smashed a few."

They continued onward through the barren landscape with only the vultures for company, or so they thought. When night fell, they set up their camp as usual and ate a small dinner consisting of a couple of rabbits Grippard had caught the day before. They did not set a watch, since they thought themselves alone in an empty land, and fell asleep quickly to be ready for an early start the next day. The lack of life in the area unnerved them and they wanted to get through as soon as possible.

Several hours later, as snores from the three tents rose into the damp, night air, a lone kralthak entered their campsite. He walked about on his hind legs, steadied by his bushy tail, and swiveled his fox head from side to side to take in the surroundings. When he was sure the camp's occupants were asleep, he called in his comrades. Now there were seven kralthaks in the campsite.

They went into Caleth's tent first. Startled awake to find two large foxes standing over him, he was too shocked to do anything to protect himself. Quazi did nothing to aid Caleth, possibly because he heard no command from him, but more likely because Quazicars were not as violent as everyone thought. Caleth was tied up without a fight and brought out to face a kralthak in the center of the camp. Flioba was taken easily as well, but apparently Grippard slept holding his war hammer. Caleth heard a startled shout and then a bone-crushing sound that sickened him to the very core. Several more kralthaks rushed in to aid their comrades, and finally Grippard was brought struggling out of his tent and lined up with Caleth and Flioba.

While standing tied up, Caleth had a chance to observe the kralthaks. They were about as tall as a man and wore tattered clothing that seemed taken from the dead bodies they found on the battlefield. These dirty rags easily revealed their gaunt forms. They wielded damaged weapons that also seemed taken from the deceased. The kralthak the captives were facing was slightly different from the others, wearing newly tailored clothing and only carrying a sheathed dagger. When the captives had settled down, he turned towards them and spoke in a deep, guttural voice.

"You have just entered my service, the Great Lord Thowgotel's," he stated and then paused, expecting bowing or kneeling at his great and mighty name. When he received no hint of subservience, he barked a command to his soldiers, who did not seem to understand the common tongue, and they pulled on the ropes binding the captives, making them fall to the ground in front of their Great Lord.

Kralthaks were not evil creatures; they just did what they had to in order to survive, which in this case meant taking the food from the campsite and capturing Caleth, Flioba, and Grippard to use as servants to grow or hunt food. However, the most important thing in kralthak society was respect, and status was very important to them. The lack of regard for the Great Lord's status was taken as a severe insult and treated as such. In fact, although the three young humans did not know it, they were actually being treated very well. If a kralthak was to disrespect his better, he would be punished severely as well as made to fall before the one he disrespected.

"Do not struggle," Thowgotel said as Grippard strained against his bonds, "I do not wish to hurt you, but I will subdue you if I must. This capture is nothing personal against you, but we are starving and have need of your supplies and services. There has not been a battle here in the last month, and without food to sustain us, we will soon perish."

Grippard glared at the Great Lord, and Thowgotel sighed. He disliked taking prisoners.

Suddenly, a giant owl swooped down out of the sky and picked up Thowgotel in its talons before rising into the air once again. Thowgotel screamed and sliced at the great, scaly talons in vain.

Caleth could not bear to watch a so obviously intelligent

creature being taken off to be eaten. The thought never passed through his head that while the kralthaks were busy watching their leader being carried off, they could make their escape. Instead, on a moment's decision, he curled his arm out away from his body in an arc to point at the owl's great back as he uttered, *"Konhekto erkto di zargath."* Quazi, still in his usual position above Caleth's shoulder, enlarged slightly, and the eternal fire gem on the chain hanging beneath his shirt glowed dimly and warmly. Seconds later, flame leapt from Caleth's fingertips in a long arc towards the owl, striking its tail feathers. A section of the tail erupted into flames, and the fire climbed in a line up the owl's back before diverging across the tops of the wings in the shape of a 'Y'.

The owl let out a startled shriek and dropped Thowgotel before flying swiftly away from the area it now associated with pain. Caleth was glad of the way his spell had turned out because he did not want to kill anything as grand and mighty as the owl, and he knew the rain would soon put out the flames.

The kralthaks rushed over to where their Great Lord was falling and grabbed a tent along the way, which they used to slow his fall as they caught him. Once he was safely on the ground, he shakily walked back over to the captives.

"Please forgive me," Thowgotel said, "I did not know you were such a powerful wizard." He turned to his soldiers and barked a command to release the prisoners, and when they had been untied, he spoke again, "You must come with us back to our den so that I may honor you as you deserve." Being a society mainly based on respect, it was very important to show respect for someone who had saved your life.

The kralthaks did not give back their weapons and supplies, and since the unbound humans did not know if they were still prisoners and just higher regarded captives, or if they had been completely freed, they agreed to go with the kralthaks back to their home.

As they made their way across the Desolate Fields, the humans became more comfortable with the kralthaks that led them. Flioba even became brave enough to ask a question she had been pondering for some time.

"I was just wondering," Flioba spoke cautiously, "you said before that your people were starving because of a lack of battles. What is there to eat when there are battles?"

"We eat whatever we can find," Thowgotel responded. "Battle zones give us numerous foods, such as the trash left behind when the fighters move on and the dead bodies of the fallen. I know that must sound horrible to you, but we do what we must to survive."

After hearing the Great Lord respond to a question that might have been viewed negatively, Caleth and Flioba began to converse with Thowgotel. Grippard would not speak, however, for he was still angry about not having his war hammer returned to him.

Chapter 6

They arrived at the entrance to the kralthak den when the night was just beginning to give way to dawn. A huge, stone door with intricate designs made by master masons rested level with the ground, guarded by two kralthaks wielding pole arms. To the side of the door was a large, wooden watchtower occupied by three kralthaks. As they approached the door, the Great Lord Thowgotel hailed the kralthaks in the watchtower and waited for all at the den entrance to nod their heads respectfully. The two at the door then pulled it open to let the Great Lord and his company pass.

"This door was built long before my time," Thowgotel informed his guests as they descended down the steps beneath it. "It was built before the war between your peoples, when this land was a forest and not a barren wilderness. In those days we did not need to live off the dead and could hunt live animals near our home and forage in the woods for berries and nuts. That is what I was told, anyway. I have never seen this land as anything but what it is now:

a land of death and destruction. We cannot even go aboveground anymore during the day, for that is when the armies march and battle. A day may come when we can return to the world of the living, but not here in this place. Too much blood has been spilled on this ground, tainting the very soil and prohibiting the growth of plant life that we all depend on."

They had entered a long hallway with worn tapestries on both sides and lit by torches in sconces along the walls. More kralthaks stood against the walls to guard in case of invasion. They walked down the hallway and passed a corridor on their right.

"That's where some of our captives attempt to grow food," Thowgotel continued, pointing down the corridor. "I don't enjoy taking captives, but there are too few of us these days, between guarding the den and searching for food. Unfortunately, even the prisoners from aboveground have difficulty getting anything edible to grow beneath the earth when the only light available is dim at best."

"Why do so many need to guard?" asked Caleth.

"People from the war are continually trying to loot our den, and as these ancient treasures are all we have, we defend them with our lives. But humans are the least of our troubles. The powerful magic used on the battlefields can become too concentrated in one place, and then sometimes the dead walk again and are horribly difficult to destroy. It is not easy to kill what is already dead. Luckily this does not happen all the time or we could not survive here."

"Why do you stay here if it is so difficult to live?" Flioba inquired.

"We know of no other place, and we cannot spare anybody to find one."

By this time, they had reached the great hall, complete with pillars, long tables, and two thrones masterfully carved out of wood and decorated with gold. They approached the thrones and made sure to bow low before the king and queen.

"Excuse me," Thowgotel spoke to his guests, "I must speak with King Filfwander Haggodsson, Ruler of the Kralthaks, Overseer of the Desolate Fields, Scavenger of the Dead, and Keeper of the Ancient Treasure: my father."

Before his guests had the chance to ask him anything about this, Thowgotel turned away and walked up to King Filfwander. He kneeled before his King and exchanged a few words in the kralthak language before returning to his feet and conversing with him. Caleth and his friends could understand none of what was said, and waited patiently until Thowgotel had finished.

Soon he returned to the group and spoke with a smile. "It is settled," he said. "We will be having dinner in a short while before our sleep through the day. During dinner, you will be rewarded properly. I shall send you with Molicia Human-Speaker to wash up before the event. She is our official translator whenever we must do business with your people." He gestured at a kralthak woman, who hurried over and exchanged a few short barks with Thowgotel. "I will see you in a bit," he told them.

"Come with me," Molicia said, and off they went towards the baths.

"If Thowgotel is the King's son, why is he the Great Lord and not the Prince?" Caleth asked on the way.

"Ah, you do not know our system of government," Molicia replied. "All kralthaks are born with the same status and must work hard to become promoted to higher and higher statuses based on occupations and accomplishments. We can also earn titles, the King has many, and these add to our prestige. The Great Lord Thowgotel has worked very diligently to reach his current standing, but he still has far to go if he wants to become King like his father. When a

King dies, those of highest standing meet to determine the new leader by weighing statuses and titles against one another. Whoever they decide has the greatest prestige will become our new King."

By this time they had reached the baths, and there they split up to wash before the meal. The kralthaks may have been starving, but they certainly had a good supply of water, which Caleth guessed came from some nearby, underground river. Soon enough, they had all finished and changed into clothes brought from their supplies. As soon as they were done, Molicia led them back to the great hall.

When they entered, they saw that ornate dishes had been set on the table and the room was now occupied by many kralthaks. However, even with the large number of them, the room still looked empty compared to the great company it must once have seated. As they walked in, Thowgotel got up from his seat at the high table and gestured for them to come over. Apparently they would sit in the seats of honor for this meal.

They walked to Thowgotel and made sure to bow low to the high table before they took their seats; it wouldn't be good to insult the kralthak leaders in their own home. Molicia sat with them in order to translate the King's words.

After they had been seated and the last few stragglers entered the great hall, the food was served. Although the serving dishes were large and well decorated, the food they contained was meager and hardly edible. Caleth didn't want to know what it was he ate, but Flioba could not help asking. To her horror, she was told that the main course was vulture with the few vegetables they had managed to grow. Thowgotel called it: "Roasted Vulture served in Red Sauce over the Vegetable of the Day." The name didn't make it sound bad, but Caleth thought to himself that it could also be called: "Week-Old Carrion Bird covered in its own Blood Sauce over Limp Roots." However, he ate the food without complaining since it tasted alright anyway, and he waited for whatever was going to happen next.

After everyone had finished the so-called dinner, although it was more like breakfast for Caleth and his friends since it was served just after the sun had risen, King Filfwander stood up. Molicia readied herself to translate what he said.

"My fellow kralthaks," the King began, "as on many days, there are a number of people to be issued new statuses. However, on this day we have a rare occurrence. As you know, we rarely confer our titles onto outsiders. But on this day, there is an outsider who shall receive one. He showed enormous respect for our people when, although just captured, he rescued his capturer from a giant owl who had snatched him in his talons. It is good to see that there are still those apart from ourselves who retain respect; too much of it has been lost...Caleth, please step forward."

Caleth rose from his seat and walked towards the King. As he got up, he heard a whispered "Remember to kneel" from Molicia. Upon reaching the King, he did as Molicia had instructed and kneeled on the ground in front of the kralthaks' leader. King Filfwander pulled a long, diamond scepter from his robe and held it over Caleth.

"Tell me your name," he commanded, first in kralthak and then in Caleth's language.

"Caleth Rictanson, my lord," Caleth replied softly.

"I, King Filfwander, confer onto the human Caleth Rictanson the title of Kralthak-Saver for his service to my people." He tapped Caleth lightly on the head and then swept the rod in a circle around Caleth's kneeling body. "Rise, Caleth Rictanson, Kralthak-Saver." Caleth got to his feet and bowed once more in front of the King. The kralthaks at the tables behind him applauded. "May you always be regarded highly," the King finished with the common kralthak phrase.

Caleth shyly returned to his seat but couldn't help a huge smile that came across his face. After he sat back down with his comrades, the King continued conferring statuses and titles on others who deserved them. In all, three kralthaks were given new statuses that night. Two were young kralthaks, and this was the first new status they had received since they were born, one being named a Guard to protect the den and the other a Scavenger to scour the battlefield for anything useful. The third kralthak was promoted from Slave Watcher to Slave Master for hearing a plot some of the captives had concocted to escape and for preventing its successful completion.

Soon the meal was over, and many of the kralthaks left to sleep for the day while others returned to their guard posts. Thowgotel led Caleth, Flioba, and Grippard to a small room where their weapons and supplies were piled on the floor. They retrieved their equipment and followed the Great Lord to the den's exit.

"Your horses will be right outside," Thowgotel stated. "Thank you again for saving my life. If you ever need our help or would like to stay with us for awhile, just tell the Kralthak Guards when you arrive at our den your title in the kralthak language, Saroofachtenel, and they will let you in without harm. May you always be regarded highly."

"May all respect your worth," Caleth replied, using the correct response this time, and then he and his companions left the kralthak den and started on the last leg of their journey to the Quantoff battle camp.

Chapter 7

The rain finally ended several hours after Caleth and his friends left the kralthak den. Cheered by this, they spurred on their mounts to greater speeds and left the Desolate Fields before nightfall. They camped in Quantoff that night, under a forest of old-growth trees. Grippard was finally talking, now that he again had the comfortable feeling of his war hammer against his back.

The next morning they rose well-rested and ready to try out their plan for infiltrating the camp. After a three hour ride, they approached the Quantoff battle camp, which was located on a grassy field bordering the forest they had just rode through. From their position on the edge of the forest, they could see the tents of the soldiers and the fire pits where they roasted their food. Lunch was just being served, and all of the camp's occupants were gathered in the center eating.

"Me an' Fred sees the book thats we be needin' to sign," Grippard spoke, pointing to a large, leather-bound volume lying open upon a pedestal near the edge of the camp, where someone should have been keeping guard and waiting for new arrivals. On a small table next to it were a quill and an inkwell. No one seemed to be paying any attention to that area of the camp, so Caleth decided it was time for them to implement their plan.

"I'll conjure a telescoping lens," Caleth stated, "and you, Flioba, can sign our names in the book. You have better distance handwriting than I do."

"I'm ready," Flioba replied.

Caleth traced a large circle in the air with his right index finger as he uttered, "*Wazak huelnef tiro visyonda.*" The circle in the air became filled with a glassy, liquid-like substance that hovered where it appeared. Anything seen through it became enlarged, though still clear.

Flioba gazed through the telescoping lens at the quill and the book. She pointed at the image of the quill as she spoke, "*Chialk flethra.*" She raised her finger and the quill lifted into the air. Then she gripped the air as she would if she was holding an actual quill and slowly moved the quill over until it was above the inkwell. She dipped it into the ink and then moved it over to the book. Then she wrote in the air, and the quill wrote their names on the page: Caleth Rictanson, Flioba Tradbensdatter, and Grippard Slactonson. After she finished, Flioba carefully returned the quill to the table and ended the spell with "*xetlan,*" a word used to cancel the most recent spell cast. Caleth did the same. They looked back over to the camp and made sure they had not been noticed. Only then could they breathe a sigh of relief.

Without further ado, they rode their horses up to the camp. As they dismounted, the man who was supposed to be keeping watch ran up. He asked for their names, and upon hearing them, marked off their arrival in the book. They encountered no trouble with the magically written names. No one had noticed. The watchman sent them off to tie up their horses and meet with someone to show them around the camp.

After they had tied up their horses to a post and left them with food and water, they were met by a tall, dark-haired man who carried a longsword in a sheath on his belt. He looked only slightly older than Grippard, who was himself only a year older than Caleth and Flioba. Flioba stared at the man in awe of his large muscles and cool demeanor. She was love-struck. Caleth saw his chances with Flioba disappear in that instant, but he put that to the back of his mind for now.

As the man approached, he greeted them. "I'm told you have just arrived," he stated. "I'm Minor Swordsmaster Lunan."

"Nice to meet you, I'm Caleth."

"Grippard an' Fred," Grippard said, hefting his war hammer.

"Wait, where's Fred?" Lunan asked. "I wasn't informed about him."

"His war hammer," Caleth mumbled.

"I see," said Lunan. "And what about you, miss?" Flioba was still staring at him and wasn't paying any attention to the conversation.

"Uh, Flioba," she stated.

"Okay," said Lunan. "It's a pleasure to meet you all. Now I'm going to show you around our camp and place you into your training group. Come with me."

Lunan pointed out all the important places in the camp, such as where they would eat, sleep, and train. After the tour, it was time to decide their training group. Quantoff did not have wizards since the Awakening spell had never been taught to anyone inside its borders, so Caleth and Flioba would have to cope with doing something they were not as good at.

"You seem to be quite proficient with your war hammer," Lunan spoke to Grippard. "I will place you in with the crushing weapons group, but you will probably be placed in the advanced group quickly, if your skills with it are truly as they seem." He next turned to Caleth. "You look like you would be good with a sword. I think I will put you in my swords group."

"That would be fine, sir," Caleth replied.

"And then there's you, Flioba," Lunan continued. "What would you like to learn?"

Flioba glanced down at Lunan's longsword. "I would like to be taught the use of the longsword," she said.

"Okay," Lunan responded, "then you'll be in the swords group with Caleth, and I shall teach you both."

◊◊◊◊◊◊◊◊

Caleth and Flioba saw little of Grippard for the rest of the day, but to be fair, Flioba saw little of anyone except Lunan. Lunan had at first given Caleth a longsword, but he quickly became exhausted just by holding it for any length of time, so Lunan instead decided to give him the type of sword many of the women used, a rapier. Caleth had a much easier time with that and picked up the techniques he was taught at a rapid pace. Flioba had a harder time using the longsword than even Caleth had had, but she was very determined and would not give up trying, especially since she wanted to impress Lunan by learning everything he had to teach her.

Also learning the use of the rapier was a beautiful girl called Granthwin, who seemed to possess uncanny luck when she dueled with others. A root would seem to reach out and trip the opponent or a sharp, spiky plant would stick through the opponent's shoe, giving her a large advantage. Caleth knew this was not luck. He could vaguely sense magic sparking off her without her knowing and creating these sudden changes to the environment around her. This was very strange since Caleth knew that few people who were not Awakened ever had stray magic leak from them, so he knew she must be very powerful, though unable to reach her full potential. To the men of Quantoff, however, and even to herself, she only looked like a fortunate girl, or a very intelligent one who would notice small details about the area where she fought and use them to her advantage.

Caleth spoke with her during a break. "You seem very skilled at the use of the rapier," he said.

"Thank you," she replied, "but it's not really any skills I have, but the mistakes of others that you see. I don't think I know your name."

"Caleth, and you are?" He didn't really need to ask since he had found out from the other pupils, but it was the polite thing to do.

"Granthwin; have you just arrived here?"

"Yes, just before lunch. I travelled with two friends, a guy and a girl. The girl's over there with Lunan. She's called Flioba. The guy is a war hammer wielder named Grippard. We had quite an adventure getting here."

"Really? What village are you from?"

"Err," Caleth hesitated, unsure of the names of Quantoff villages. "Well, I can't really say I'm from one specific village. You see, my mother and father travel around a lot. They're merchants who buy things in one village and sell it for a higher price in another where the demand is higher. I've seen a fair number of Quantoff's villages, but I can't truly call any one my home."

"Well that has to be an interesting life. I never did any travelling in my youth. I was needed at my parents' work. They own a tavern called The Steel Mule. There are always things that need doing, that's for sure."

Then the break was over, and Caleth was luckily spared from coming up with any more details about his false family and young life. They were kept training until dinner, and only then did Caleth and Flioba see Grippard again. He had an enormous grin plastered on his face and ate ravenously. Apparently, a little weapons training was all he needed to be happy.

They talked a little as they waited in line for their dinners, but after they received their food, they dispersed to various places. Flioba went off to sit with Lunan, and Grippard sat with a bunch of his new friends from the crushing weapons group. Seeing his companions abandon him, Caleth dejectedly sat down by himself.

Caleth sadly sat alone with only Quazi for company, although that was hardly any company at all since Quazi slept in Caleth's pocket, and they couldn't communicate with each other anyway. Caleth would have to keep Quazi hidden while he was in the Quantoff camp so as not to arouse suspicion. The food was horrible, as Caleth had suspected it would be; however, it was edible, and he was starving after the physical exertion of the day.

Halfway through the meal, Caleth was joined by Granthwin, who had noticed that he had no one to sit with, and soon Lunan and Flioba joined him as well, though it looked as if that was not Flioba's idea. They talked of the war, and Caleth was surprised to find out that Lunan disapproved of it. Apparently he disliked killing people, although "it's not like the Jokatonans are really people," as he put it. The children of Quantoff had been taught from a young age that the people of Jokatone were bloodthirsty brutes who could manipulate the very elements to destroy.

Caleth had never heard such stories of violence and evil, such as the mutilation of Quantoff babies and the burning of towns with people still in the buildings. It made him wonder if he was on the wrong side of the war. Did his people cover up these incidents so they would not look bad, or were these just fabrications to instill a rage towards the people of Jokatone?

Chapter 8

The next few weeks passed in a constant routine of training, breaking for meals, and sleeping. Caleth used only minor spells to make his time there a little more convenient, and these were used only when he thought no one else was looking. He had become quite proficient with the rapier and a good friend of Granthwin, with whom he had taken to training with. Together they had become the most skilled pair of rapier wielders in the camp, and were even recognized by the Master Swordsmaster for their abilities.

During this time, Flioba had become very close to Lunan, and they now did everything together. Grippard had advanced far quicker than most had thought possible. He was already almost a Minor Crushmaster. However, the amount of time they spent training left little to discuss anything they might have heard. They knew almost nothing about the Quantoffans' next plan of attack until they were already involved in it.

After days of calm monotony, a messenger suddenly arrived in the camp one morning. The Camp Leader listened to the news he brought and was handed a small scroll. After reading it silently to himself, his scarred face broke out into a crooked smile with missing teeth.

"Looks like we've finally got a job to do," he said softly, as if to himself.

Then he called everyone to the center of the camp to tell them of their next assignment. They were tasked with raiding a Jokatone town. Caleth was not exactly sure what this entailed, but it didn't sound good. He wondered how he would escape to tell the Head Caster before the Quantoff battle party reached its destination. It didn't seem that he would be given a chance.

As soon as the Camp Leader made his announcement, everyone began frantically preparing for departure. Caleth helped take down the tents and bundle everything onto the horses. It was a grueling process. They finished slightly after lunch, and then began the long walk to Jokatone. No one was able to ride, since all the horses had been needed to carry supplies.

The walk was easy enough, taking them back the way Caleth and his companions had come; this time Caleth could talk to Granthwin as a diversion. He felt it was a very pleasant walk, although he was always looking for an opportunity to meet up with Flioba and Grippard to discuss some sort of plan. This never happened, however, since Flioba would not be dragged away from Lunan's side and Grippard was too excited about the possibility of using his war hammer to be coherent.

Soon they had to stop for the night, but they unpacked only the barest minimum, avoiding having to re-pack everything the next day. Even after the day's exercise, they still trained before sleeping. Training had become almost fun for Caleth because it distracted him from his thoughts. He still did not know what to do about his orders from the Head Caster, and none of his original companions would spend any time talking with him. They seemed to have forgotten the Head Caster's orders altogether.

The next day, as the battle party walked slowly through the forest, Caleth spoke with Granthwin about the mission.

"Are you ready for this raid?" Caleth asked.

"Sure, I guess so," replied Granthwin, "but I'm a little nervous. This is my first real assignment, and I hope I can actually live up to others' expectations."

"I'm sure you'll be fine, but how are we going to go about this raid?"

"I assume we'll sneak up on them and kill them in their sleep."

Caleth grimaced mentally. This wasn't something he wanted to be involved in. "Why are we killing them anyway?"

"Because they're murderers, of course; if we don't kill them, they'll kill us."

"I don't think they're killing anyone at this point. It's not like they're in the Jokatone army anymore."

"What do you mean? I thought all Jokatonans were completely determined to destroy us. How do you know this anyway?"

Caleth winced at his slip. Now she might suspect he wasn't really a Quantoffan. "Uh, my parents and I came upon a band of older Jokatonans when we were traveling. At first, we were wary and thought they would kill us, but they offered us their campfire instead. We learned a great deal from them."

Granthwin didn't buy it, but she didn't press the matter. "Are you telling me that these people we are going to raid are just like our own relatives back home?"

"Well, yeah. Apparently both Jokatone and Quantoff follow similar plans concerning the lives of their people. Everyone grows

up to a certain age, then they fight for a while, and finally they
settle down to live out their lives doing other jobs necessary for a
kingdom's economic stability. How else would the Jokatonans get
food, and weapons, and such? Someone has to take care of that. Not
everyone can fight in any society."

"You know," Granthwin spoke hesitantly, "you may be right.
I've never thought of that before."

They went on for a while in silence, each lost in their own
thoughts. Finally, Caleth and Granthwin began speaking again and
continued to converse until they entered the Desolate Fields, when
an ominous silence fell over the entire company.

Their time in the Desolate Fields passed slowly, each moment
dragging on for what felt like an eternity. Caleth noticed a few
kralthaks on the edge of his vision, but they were intelligent enough
to stay away from the battle party. Each night, the Quantoffans
ordered a large number of soldiers to be on guard duty. The
landscape looked empty, but there was a feeling of unnatural evil in
the air.

One night, although the landscape was as barren and lifeless as
ever, something rose upwards and stood like a man in the gloom. It
approached the camp slowly and with a stiff gait. Unsure of what it
was, the sentries alerted the rest of the battle party. As it
approached the light of the camp, its figure could be made out.
Although it looked like it might once have been a man, this
abomination was a man no longer. In many places, its flesh had
rotted away and its bones were visible. Its head was just a skull, and
its eye sockets were empty; however, it somehow was aware of the
camp and its occupants. The air around it was fetid and caused
retching among the soldiers.

Caleth could feel the intense concentration of magic
surrounding the undead creature. He thought that this must be one

of the dead things the kralthaks had mentioned. The magic allowed it to sense the presence of the people and let it stand upright. This was the consequence of the horrible spells that had been cast on the battlefield. The remnants of the sorcery had gathered together and brought forth this abomination from its endless sleep.

Caleth unsheathed his rapier and saw the rest of the company take out their own respective weapons, but he knew the only truly effective weapon would be magic. However, he could not risk giving away his identity, so he had to cope just like everybody else.

When the hideous creature reached the edge of the encampment, the soldiers charged. Caleth and Granthwin worked as a fully functioning team, but their stabs and slashes had no affect on the monster. It seemed the only people who could actually do anything were those from the crushing weapons group. This did not keep the others from trying, however. Lunan slashed the abomination's head off its shoulders, but neither the head nor the body seemed weakened. The skull fell towards a woman's arm and clenched onto her with its teeth, causing her to scream and fall backwards onto the ground in agony. A man with a maul attempted to help her by smashing the top of the skull to dust, but even without being attached to the head, the jaws continued to clench. It took two strong men to wrench them apart. Grippard managed to smash one of the creature's arms, but still it ripped at people with the other. The creature's magic was strong.

Eventually, the members of the crushing weapons group managed to obliterate the creature, but even the parts that were left seemed evil and intent on murder. Several people were ordered to take them out away from the camp and bury them. After a long, hard-fought battle, the company had defeated the abomination. There was only one major injury, the one from the jaw, but even the scratches could be a problem if infection took hold, and without magic, this was always a possibility.

Caleth went with the people who were to bury the parts and told them that he would bury them and they could just go back. They gratefully accepted and left Caleth with the remains of the creature. Caleth wanted to be sure the foul magic was gone, and he couldn't have anyone watching him.

First, he tried a simple Cancel spell. "*Xetlan hre awanin kli,*" he muttered. Nothing happened. The magic was too concentrated. Realizing this, he decided to use a Major Cancel spell and whispered, "*Ri xetlan hre awanin kli.*" Still there was no change in the dark magic he sensed. Caleth sighed; it looked as if he would have to use a much more potent and specific spell. This time he traced an area surrounding the repulsive bits and uttered, "*Eknadon hre awanin kli dua fornijka kli hre naual di panthuanto.*" This was a much more draining spell meant to heal the area Caleth had traced and counteract the undead's awakening. This time, he felt a change. A soft breeze caressed his face as it blew across the Desolate Fields, and it carried off the tainted magic as it passed.

Caleth felt relieved but was now exhausted. He turned back towards the camp to make sure no one had noticed his spellcasting. All looked well, but he thought he saw Granthwin staring towards him. His heart leapt into his throat at the thought of being caught, but she turned away without seeming to notice anything amiss. Now all Caleth had to do was bury the pieces.

Soon Caleth was back in the camp, attempting to get a few more hours of sleep before they started off again. He could finally relax. The evil, lurking feeling was gone.

Chapter 9

After days of travel in fair weather, the battle party reached the Jokatone border. From there, it was only a day's ride where the raid would take place, a town with the name of Briktal. Caleth knew it was an average-sized town on the edge of a large lake. Most of the fish eaten in the battle school had come from there. If he recalled correctly, few spellcasters lived in this particular town. The only one he knew of for sure was the healer; all the rest of the townspeople were retired soldiers.

The Quantoffan battle party set up camp inside the border in a place where they could not be easily noticed by the Jokatonans, but where they would be close enough to mount a raid. There they trained for long hours before receiving their last-minute instructions. As they readied for their attack, the sky grew dark and storm clouds formed overhead.

When night fell, the soldiers marched as quietly as they could to Briktal and surrounded it once they arrived. Then they listened for their signal. Caleth's job was to stand outside the houses in the street and kill off anyone who happened to flee. He was accompanied by the other newcomers to the camp, namely Granthwin, Grippard, and Flioba, who had apparently been forcibly separated from Lunan, among others. Caleth's time was running out, and he could not find a way to escape. It was too late now anyway; by the time he made it back to the battle school and told the Head Caster, all of the people would already be dead.

The town stood in eerie silence, as if awaiting its own destruction. Its inhabitants were sleeping, suspecting nothing, and even the dogs had not yet caught wind of the Quantoffans. The streets lay empty in the dark, and the houses cast long, barely-visible shadows in the light of the moon. The Quantoffans were ready to strike.

Suddenly, the soldiers began to race down into the town. The signal must have been given, but Caleth missed it while wandering in his thoughts. As he watched, he was surprised to see that Grippard had gone with them for some unknown reason. What was going on? Caleth knew that Grippard was supposed to wait with the rest of the camp's newcomers.

All of a sudden, Caleth saw Grippard outrace those around him and abruptly turn, smashing into the soldiers rushing down the hill. He bellowed a war cry as he swung his war hammer into the ranks of those around him, wreaking havoc wherever he swung. Caleth heard voices in the crowd.

"He's gone mad!" someone shouted.

"What's going on?" another asked.

"Quick, take him out before he wakes the townspeople!" one of the weapons masters cried.

However, it was too late. The townspeople began emerging from their homes, and when they realized what was going on, they hurriedly grabbed their weapons from their younger days and fought to defend their town.

Meanwhile, Grippard was being attacked on all sides by the Quantoffans. They cursed him for his actions and attempted to slaughter him where he stood. Caleth didn't know what to do. He winced as the first screams reached his ears, and the soldiers spilled around Grippard to combat the Jokatonans. Was there no way he could end this blood bath? Flioba looked stunned, and Lunan too was hovering on the edge of the fray. Granthwin stood watching Caleth, wondering what he would do. She had no wish to participate in this battle when things had gone so horribly wrong.

Soon, people on both sides were falling around their comrades, but Grippard still stood, a testament to his strength and skill with the war hammer. However, he was badly beaten and was bleeding from a dozen wounds. Amongst the slaughter, Caleth saw a young girl rush in tears to her dying mother's side.

Suddenly, great emotions welled up in Caleth as he saw a Quantoffan swing his weapon towards her. The Quantoffans had said that the Jokatonans were monsters, but here was proof that the Quantoffans were just as bad, if not worse, than their enemies. Caleth acted without thinking. He could not let this atrocity happen. His body arched, flinging his face skyward as his arms flung out on either side, and he uttered in a deep voice, filled with pain and sorrow, *"Konhekto fachalan ji draktoneth masu kua kena da hikuanix lir masos nakan jinakan."* He did not know where these words came from, some of them he knew, but others he could not remember being taught. As the last word left his lips, the tremendous power of the spell caused Quazi to sense it even buried deep in Caleth's pocket, and he expanded until he burst forth into the open air, adding further strength to the spell. Seconds later, as Caleth stood motionless in concentration, a bolt of lightning raced down from the clouds above and split directly over Caleth's head into many bolts of pure electrical power that shot out towards those involved in the battle.

One man on the battlefield noticed Caleth's spellcasting and threw his spear towards him with all his strength in an attempt to silence him and stop the spell, but it was already too late. The bolts of lightning struck nearly everyone on the battlefield, leaving only Grippard, Granthwin, Flioba, and Lunan, along with the children, still standing. All those who had participated in the horrible skirmish, with the sole exception of Grippard, lay motionless on the ground. Flioba noticed as the spear arched towards Caleth, and she reacted instantly casting out her hand towards him and rapidly speaking, "*Konhekto hethwaf de slana do suelnak tiro kua bolkef.*"

A dome of ice grew up around Caleth and glinted in the light of the moon. The spear hurtled towards it and struck with a crash. The hastily constructed dome shattered, but it had done what was needed, halting the progress of the spear. Caleth was safe. Flioba watched his face turn towards her. His eyes were oddly glowing bright white and shone in the darkness. Then the light disappeared, and Caleth collapsed on the ground.

Moments later, he rose, looking as if nothing had happened. Apparently Quazi had taken most of the strain himself, and now he lay unmoving, but alive. Caleth placed him in a different pocket.

Granthwin and Lunan were staring at Caleth and Flioba with a mixture of shock and fear, with a little awe thrown in. The children were not wasting any time. After finding that the people were not dead, they quickly began dragging their town's wounded to the healer, who had not left her house during the fighting, waiting for the aftermath where she could be more useful and less likely killed. The old woman began her task at once while her patients were still stunned and out cold.

"Would you mind telling us what's going on?" Granthwin asked Caleth.

"Err, I guess I might as well tell you now," he replied. "Flioba, Grippard, and I..." he glanced down at Grippard to see the man calmly dragging the Quantoffan bodies into the forest, "are not really from Quantoff."

"Well, no shock there," Granthwin interjected. "Continue."

"We were sent by the Head Caster of the Jokatone battle school to infiltrate your camp and bring word of your plans. However, we were unable to drift off back to the battle school, so we were forced to come with you. When I saw your people begin to slaughter the children, I realized that the Quantoffans were just as bad as your tales of the Jokatonans. I couldn't stand idly by during this horrible blood bath, so I put an end to it." He left out the part of it being completely unintentional.

"Why were we not stunned as well?" Lunan inquired.

"I noticed that you both held back during the battle. You didn't seem quite as thrilled about participating." Caleth made up the reason. He didn't really know why they had been spared. He hadn't specifically excluded them from his spell. The only parameter was that the lightning was to strike enemies; he guessed they somehow didn't fit in the enemy category.

"Well now how are we going to go back to our people?!" Lunan exclaimed. "We will be considered traitors and punished accordingly!"

"I'm really sorry. I didn't mean for this to happen, any of it really. Maybe you can come back with us to our school. With luck they might accept you."

"Hmm, I don't know," Lunan spoke. "I'm not interested in siding with the enemy."

"I think I will join you," Granthwin stated. "It will be

interesting to see how this whole thing plays out."

"Come on Lunan," Flioba pressured. "We're really not that bad."

"I guess I have no choice," Lunan decided. "I will come."

They turned back to help with the bodies. They needed to get them far enough apart so that the early risers would not instantly slaughter their stunned opponents. Surprisingly, Grippard had already finished.

He was standing near the edge of the town on the opposite side of where they came in, and he beckoned for them to join him as he melded into the forest. Confused, Caleth and his companions did as he bade and soon met up with him beneath the gloomy boughs of the trees. He turned to face them.

"There is something I must show you," he said, in a voice uncharacteristically not his own and without his usual dialect.

As Caleth, Granthwin, Flioba, and Lunan watched, Grippard's figure became darker, until it was nearly impossible to make out his features in the shadows of the trees. Then his form began to blur and distort. He grew in size until he towered over them, and then his form began to substantiate. He was no longer the Grippard they had known. He was now a dragon with bronze-tinted scales, whose inner light shone out upon the forest floor, brightening the night. Majestic wings unfurled behind him and a long tail snaked its way around the forest floor. The humans beneath him stood in confusion and shock, but also felt wonder at gazing upon such a magnificent creature.

"Caleth, you saved my life, or at least you would have if I was human," the dragon spoke, "so now I show you my true form. Please, allow me to explain. I never was the Grippard you thought you were traveling with. My true name is Hranthus, and I am the King of Jokatone. I went to the battle school with the intent of finding people who would be worthy of joining my elite force, a group that is tasked with all missions I deem most important. When the Head Caster commanded me to join you on this assignment, I was certain that this would take away time that would be put to better use observing the majority of the pupils. Apparently this was not the case. I would like to offer you a position on my elite force."

"Um," Caleth replied, "I'll have to think about it. Why did you go with the Quantoffans all the way to Briktal without slipping away to warn the Jokatonans?"

"I thought that I could easily have dispatched the Quantoffans by myself. I am very powerful even in human form. I would have killed them all anyway, if I had had more time. Of course, it would have been much easier if I had just transformed back into a dragon, but I dislike having people know who I truly am."

"I see," said Caleth, feeling uncomfortable. "I'm just wondering…" Caleth started.

"Yes…" Hranthus waited.

"Why are we fighting this war anyway?"

"Well, you see Caleth," Hranthus answered. "All people need a purpose. War gives them one. It gives them a reason to live, to get up in the morning. Without this war, the people would have no motivation. They live their lives as best they can to get back at their opponents for the cruelties they believe they have inflicted. The war isn't for anything, Caleth. No one is ever supposed to win. The king of Quantoff is actually a good friend of mine, and we came up with this plan a long time ago to solve the problem of laziness."

"But if the war has no objective," Caleth reasoned, "then the people have no purpose anyway. They are not truly fighting for anything."

"The purpose of the war is purpose itself. I will talk no longer about this subject. What is your decision?"

"I cannot accept your offer," Caleth responded. "I do not accept the premise of the war, and it hurts me to think of the meaningless cruelty inflicted upon so many people for no reason whatsoever. People don't need war to live."

"I am sorry to hear that is your decision. Regardless of your feelings about the war, I am indebted to you. If you ever need anything, come to me and I will see what I can do."

With that being said, Hranthus took off into the air and circled once overhead before flying off. Caleth wondered if he would ever see him again, and if he ever wanted to. The whole discussion of war had shaken him.

"Well," Lunan spoke, "what now?"

"I guess we will be going to the battle school," Caleth answered, "though we will have to make up some excuse for Grippard's absence."

They left Briktal and made their way back to the battle school. No one spoke much. No one knew what to say. They all felt rather weird and uncomfortable about their situation, but they had to go on. What else was there to do?

Chapter 10

They finally reached the battle school after several long days. Their clothes were ragged and dirty, since they had left their packs with the Quantoffans and had not gone back. They were forced to stop at villages along the way to get food, but they managed. They approached the entrance with relief, but were stopped by guards before they could pass through.

"They can't come in," one of the guards spoke, gesturing towards Lunan and Granthwin.

"Sure they can," Caleth replied, annoyed. "They're with me. I'll go talk to Head Caster Glantius about it immediately."

"They cannot enter," the guard repeated, "and the Head Caster wants to speak to you only. They will wait for you outside."

"I'll stay with them," Flioba offered.

"Fine," stated Caleth. "I'll be back as quick as I can."

He walked rapidly into the battle school and towards the tower. He wanted to get this over with as quickly as possible so they could all get some clean clothes and some good food. As he rode the staircase, he thought of what he would say. However, when he entered the Head Caster's room, it seemed he wouldn't be doing much of the talking.

"Caleth!" Head Caster Glantius shouted. "You are a failure! I assigned you an easy mission, just get in and get out! Could you not even do that?!"

"Uh…" Caleth started.

"And now you bring back those evil Quantoffans here to the battle school?! What are you thinking?!"

"I can explain…"

"And where's Grippard?! He was one of our finest fighters! Did you get him killed?!"

"No, sir. He left us."

"And for good reason! Tramping around with those demons!"

"Begging your pardon, sir, but how do you know how my assignment went?"

"You think I can't cast a Clairvoyance spell?! You really want to insult me after you already botched your assignment?!"

"No, sir; I'm sorry, sir."

"You had better be! You won't be doing another assignment for a long time! And go tell your little friends to go home!"

"But, sir…they could help us. They're good fighters, and the girl seems like she could be an excellent wizard. She has such strong magic that it leaks from her."

"Are you kidding?! Awaken a Quantoffan?! No, they must leave, or I'll have them killed!"

"I can't stand for that, sir. You have to let them stay."

"Telling me what to do now, huh?! Well you know what?! You're banished! Leave Jokatone and never return!"

"I'm sorry you feel that way, sir. You know, for being the Head

Caster, you have no idea of what's going on in this war."

Caleth left without waiting for a reply. He was incredibly angry, but he was worried as well. How could he survive away from civilization? His spells could only help so much. He didn't know enough of the language of magic to truly live using only spellcasting. It would be a hard life.

Banishment was the most feared punishment a Jokatonan could receive. To the north, an enormous canyon shattered all hopes of crossing; to the west, endless forest stretched as far as the eye could see and were filled with dangerous creatures; to the south, Quantoff would kill any Jokatonan; and to the east, endless plains were inhabited by the fiercest demons known. There was no sanctuary for the banished.

As he left the tower, Caleth decided to stop by Master Spellblender Trifus to see if he could help. Master Trifus was sitting in his room going over notes on what he would be teaching the next day. Caleth approached him.

"Master Trifus," Caleth spoke, "is there any way you can help me?"

"With what, my dear boy?" Master Trifus responded. He was very fond of Caleth.

Caleth told Master Trifus the whole story, and when he reached the end, Master Trifus agreed to help him. Caleth was given a book of magic words. It would assist, but it could only hold so much. Caleth was relieved that he had received anything, and before he left, Master Trifus gave him advice.

"Stay off the paths as you leave Jokatone," he stated. "Glantius will have distributed notices by tomorrow that you are to be killed on sight. He hates when people talk back to him, and loathes when someone tells him what to do. I'm sure you'll be fine, though. Good luck out there."

A Broken World

Caleth left Master Trifus and returned to his companions. They looked at him expectantly, but unfortunately the only news he brought was bad. Surprisingly, they agreed to accompany him in his banishment, but Caleth informed them that he wasn't planning to leave Jokatone quite yet. He had another plan in mind: he was going to ask a favor of Hranthus.

Chapter 11

They set off at once, trying to get as far as possible from the battle school before night fell. They trudged through small forests and long fields, attempting to stay away from inhabited areas. Unfortunately, they had no food, but they were at least able to stop at small streams to refill their canteens. It was difficult to hunt for food without a ranged weapon, and they couldn't use magic because Caleth had cast a Magic Concealment spell over the group in order to prevent the Head Caster from locating them. Any spells cast at this point would give away their position.

They managed to find some berries the next day to ease their hunger slightly, but it wasn't much. Later on, Lunan managed to find a bird's nest, and they ate the eggs. Still they needed more to eat, and they knew they would need it soon. After arguing for a while, they decided they would have to steal food from the next town they came to, although they didn't feel good about resorting to such measures.

A Broken World

Just after what should have been lunch, Caleth and his companions reached the town of Vinimir. They decided to wait for nightfall before attempting their theft. Unfortunately, there was little cover around the town, just a few small bushes and scattered trees, but it would have to do, and they hoped they would not be noticed.

After the sun sank below the horizon and they could see the silhouettes of the people leave the streets and return to their homes, it was time to begin. Since the robbery was Caleth's idea, they made him be the one to go through with it. The rest would wait on the outskirts of the town and help if need be. They all hoped he wouldn't need help.

Caleth set off cautiously, not wishing to make any loud noises that might give away his presence. He scanned the signs in the gloom, attempting to find a bakery, butcher shop, or any other such store. For a while, he had no luck, but eventually he noticed a sign that read "The Lofty Loaf." Figuring that this would be a bakery, Caleth tried the door, but to no avail. It was locked. Unable to unlock it without magic, he wondered whether he should break the window to enter, but that would make too much noise. He then remembered that bakeries made new bread every day, and had to do something with the bread that didn't sell. He decided to look around the back for a waste heap, and to his relief, there was one. It was a nasty task digging the discarded bread out from the other refuse, but they could pick off the bad parts later.

Caleth felt better after collecting the bread and placing it into a sack. Now at least they had something to eat, even if it wasn't very appetizing. He continued to search until he found "Dravel and Sons" with a picture of a chicken breast beneath the name. Looking through the window, he salivated at the large array of meats hanging from the ceiling. The door to this shop was locked as well.

69

Disheartened, Caleth turned away, but then he thought of an idea. It wasn't a very well-thought out plan, but he could try. He let Quazi out of his pocket and watched as the creature slowly rose into the air. Quazi was glowing dimly, but Caleth didn't think he let off enough magic to disturb the Magic Concealment spell. Although he wasn't sure if Quazi could understand him, Caleth whispered his intentions to him anyway. He told Quazi that he wanted him to enter the lock and expand until he pushed the tumblers into their unlocked positions. Then he was to turn until the lock clicked open.

Seeming to understand his thoughts, if not necessarily his words, Quazi did as Caleth bade. There was a click, and Caleth tried the door. It opened. Caleth smiled at his plan's success. Deciding to go back to the bakery after he was finished here, he stealthily entered the butcher shop and purloined some of the meats, placing them carefully into his bag. He didn't want to take too many and put the butcher out of business, but he had to eat.

Soon, he finished and left the shop as quietly as he had entered, pulling the door shut behind him. Quazi attempted to fly up to the spot he often occupied over Caleth's shoulder, but Caleth quickly shoved him back in his pocket before the glow drew unwanted attention. But it was too late; he had been seen by a man exiting the local tavern.

"Wha' are you doin' nea' Dravel's shop?" the man slurred. He stumbled a little as he waited for a response. Then suddenly he shouted, "Hey, I knows you! Youse the man on the wanted posta!" He yelled back to the tavern, "Hey guys! I foun' the wanted man!"

Caleth bolted. He knew he could outrun the drunken man, but he didn't want to risk being chased by everyone else. He got out of town as fast as he could, and when he reached his comrades, they didn't ask any questions. They all ran until they were as far away from the town as their legs could take them, and stopping only once the lone sound in the still, night air was that of their own heavy breathing. It looked like they had escaped for the moment, but news of the sighting would travel fast. Soon the Head Caster would know where they had been. They would have to hurry onwards towards their destination.

They walked on farther after they had caught their breath, and then finally made camp along a stream where they could fill their canteens and make a roaring fire to cook some of the meat. Luckily for them, the group was far enough away from surrounding villages so that their fire was not spotted, and ate better than they had in weeks. Their only hope was that the bread did not have any grime still clinging that could cause sickness.

After the meal, Caleth spent time studying the book he had been given. Unfortunately, it wasn't very large, but it covered many of the common magic words that he might need once he left Jokatone. He only hoped it would suffice.

As he slowly memorized the words, Granthwin came over to sit beside him. Caleth thought of how beautiful she looked in the light of the fire, but he didn't say anything. After watching him for a while, Granthwin spoke.

"So why are we going to King Hranthus anyway?" she asked.

Caleth hesitated for a moment. "For you," he eventually said.

"I don't understand," Granthwin stated, confused. "What does this have to do with me?"

"Well," Caleth slowly started. He wasn't sure how she would react to what he had to say. "You see, you actually have great magical potential that is just waiting to be Awakened."

"What?!" Granthwin gasped in shock.

"It's true," Caleth continued. "I can sense the magic leaking off of you even as we speak. Haven't you ever wondered about the little incidents when you're dueling? The roots that stick out and

71

seem to trip people on purpose? There's a reason for that. Anyone who has potential for magic has trace amounts of it leak off of them before they are Awakened, but for most people it is undetectable. However, in your case, the magic is quite strong. Take a look at that blueberry bush." He pointed. At the moment, the bush was bare of fruit, most likely due to hungry birds.

Caleth went on, "Right now, I can sense a blob of magic that you leaked streaking out towards that bush. Watch it carefully." Granthwin did as Caleth bade. Right before their eyes, the bush suddenly grew a berry, which quickly ripened until it was a deep blue.

"I did that?!" Granthwin exclaimed softly. "But how?"

"Just stray magic doing whatever it will," Caleth answered. "Most of the time you don't notice anything, and when you do, you often rationalize it by thinking that you just didn't happen to notice it before. Go and pick the berry. It probably tastes quite good."

Granthwin retrieved it and popped it into her mouth. "Mm, it's delicious," she said as she swallowed it.

"You seem to have a natural affinity for earth magic. As far as I have seen, all of the magic you have leaked has affected only plants."

"If you can sense this magic," Granthwin inquired, "then can't Flioba sense it as well?"

"I'm not sure," Caleth answered. "Magic works differently for different people. There are those who can sense magic, but others do not even know it is possible. I think if she had sensed your leaked magic, she probably would have said something."

"Wait, what does this have to do with Hranthus?"

"I am going to ask him to Awaken you. There are few who know how, and fewer still who are willing to do it."

"You don't mind if I tell Lunan and Flioba about this, do you?" Granthwin asked.

"No, go ahead. They should know of our mission."

Granthwin left Caleth to his studies and went to tell the others. Her head was spinning, and she wondered what this all meant. What would it be like to wield the very elements at your command?

Chapter 12

After seven more days, Hranthus' castle was finally visible on the horizon. They wished that they had taken horses when they left Briktal so that they could have had an easier journey. However, they would have been more conspicuous if they had them. The food they had taken from Vinimir was running low, and they would soon need new provisions, not to mention new clothes, since they had not had clean ones since they left the Quantoffan battle party. They slept, hoping that the next day would bring an end to the misery of their journey thus far.

The following morning, they rose early and started towards the castle in high spirits. It took them more than half the day to reach its base. As they gazed upon the massive gate, they realized that they now had a problem. They had forgotten about the guards. How could they manage to get past them without being noticed? They wondered whether the guards or the wizards were the worst problem. After discussing it for a time, they settled on using magic.

At least then, it would take time for the wizards to appear, and they could possibly have finished their business with Hranthus before they arrived.

In the back of Caleth's book, there were a few sample spells. He had noticed that one of them was an Invisibility spell, which would work well in this situation. However, it was complicated and involved blending different elemental magics. Caleth thought he could manage it, though, so he prepared for the incantation. It would be a straining experience.

Before the spell was cast, they gathered a short distance away from the castle, not wanting to draw any attention. Caleth instructed them to stand in a circle and each place their left hand into the middle to create a stack with Caleth's hand on the bottom. He then made sure Quazi was out of his pocket and picked up a few stray leaves with his right hand. He began to speak as he tossed the leaves into the air and swung his right hand out away from the center of the circle. He uttered, *"Konhekto panthuanto ji lesthra oniquon kua krelp yitox nakan visyonda di suelnak do panthuerno ji futa."* He felt the presence of magic at work in his mind, and Quazi swelled. The leaves began to swirl around their group as the winds picked up. The leaves began to revolve around them faster and faster until they became a blur, and Caleth and his companions could see a fluid-like dome encasing them. The leaves shot out, and the dome thickened slightly. The exterior of the dome was slowly revolving around the group, but Caleth felt that the spell had been completed.

The group began to walk towards the castle, and as they did so, the dome moved with them. At first, they approached cautiously, but when they were certain that the guards could not see them, they began to relax. Soon, they were walking up to the open gate. They went right by the guards out front, but they remained unnoticed.

As soon as Caleth walked beneath the gate, a massive pressure slammed down on his mind. He stumbled, but caught himself and kept moving, though it was painful. Quazi fainted. Caleth managed to place Quazi in his pocket and continue on a bit farther, but the pressure was unbearable. The only reason Caleth could think of for Quazi to faint and for the rest of his group to remain unhindered was that something was attacking the Invisibility spell.

Caleth could take the pain no longer. He stumbled past the guards on the other side of the gate and then let go of his grasp on the spell. The dome disappeared in an instant, and Caleth fell to the ground. Visible once again, they were soon spotted by the guards. One approached.

"We've been expecting you," he said.

Caleth didn't find this very reassuring. He rose to his feet.

"King Hranthus has been waiting for you all," the man continued. "Follow me."

The guard immediately began walking off towards the center of the castle. Without knowing what else to do, Caleth and his companions followed. Before they were taken to Hranthus they were first given baths and new clothes to appear presentable before the King. Unbelievably happy that this was the case and feeling much better after being cleaned up and dressed in fresh clothes, they could now deal with whatever came their way. Caleth couldn't enjoy this as much as the others, however, because his head was still throbbing.

Soon they were taken before the King. Hranthus was seated in his human form, making Caleth and his friends feel more comfortable. They prostrated themselves in front of him in a sign of respect, and Hranthus bade them to rise. He then began to speak.

"I see that we meet again," Hranthus stated. "You appear to have had the worst of fortunes. You must be starving. After this meeting, you must have food before you leave."

"It is good to see you again," Caleth greeted him, "and we would be grateful for your food."

"All in due time," Hranthus said. "First, tell me why you have come."

"Caleth was banished," Lunan spoke up. "The wizards are after us, and the whole country is out for blood."

"So I have heard," Hranthus responded, "but do not fear. Here there is safety from magic, as you certainly found out when you entered." He turned to Caleth.

"What was that?" Caleth asked.

"My own little spell," Hranthus replied. "Just an Anti-Magic spell, don't they teach you those in school?"

"Well, somewhat," Caleth responded, "but definitely nothing that powerful..."

"I'm surprised you held your spell as long as you did," Hranthus told him. "You must be quite the powerful spellcaster yourself. Although you did have help, of course." He glanced pointedly at the bulge in Caleth's pocket.

"But enough of this," Hranthus continued. "Why have you come? I assume you would like to ask a favor and thereby cancel my debt to you."

"It is as you have said," Caleth replied. "We need a favor. Granthwin, here," he gestured towards her, "seems to have great magical potential, but I cannot find someone who will Awaken her. Could you do it?"

"Nay," Hranthus responded, "I do not possess that knowledge, but I can tell you where to find someone who does. It will be good, for without the battle school you will have no purpose, and a journey will give you one. I will tell you where to find the one who Awakened me. She is an ancient gold dragon, great and wise. I know not how long she has lived, but she was here many ages before men settled in Jokatone or Quantoff."

"Is this the same golden dragon who taught the Spell of Awakening to the first wizard?" Flioba interrupted.

"I seem to recall that, yes," Hranthus answered. "Marinteya the All-Knowing, she is called, for few possess greater knowledge than she. She lives in the Shield Mountains, deep inside a cave in the largest peak, the only one with snow permanently upon its summit."

"We will find this cave," Caleth spoke confidently.

"I'm sure you will," Hranthus replied, "but when you meet her, speak carefully. She had a falling-out with humans a long time ago. And do not use the word 'dragon' in her presence. That is the name humans gave us. Originally, we were called vashakax, which was the plural for vashaka."

"If it pleases her, we will use this word," Caleth assured him.

"Good," Hranthus spoke, "then it is time to eat."

Hranthus rose and led the company into a private dining room. While they ate with a vengeance, he looked over maps with them and directed them on the best routes. After much discussion and after finally filling their stomachs, they decided to travel just outside of Jokatone's eastern border in the Endless Plains until they passed Jokatone's southern border and then take the safer route through Quantoff. According to Lunan and Granthwin, they would not be hunted in Quantoff, although they couldn't linger for fear of being recognized as war deserters. Granthwin suggested that they stop at her family's tavern, The Steel Mule, to replenish supplies since it was on the southernmost edge of Quantoff, just before the beginning of the hills that led to the Shield Mountains.

They agreed on this plan, and then spent time preparing for their departure on the following morning. Hranthus had generously offered the use of his spare rooms for the night, and they could not refuse since these might be the last beds they would sleep on in a long while. Hranthus provided supplies and the food for their journey. He was surprisingly helpful, but he cheerfully told them it was all part of repaying the debt he owed to Caleth, though they doubted this was the case. Maybe he was just pleased to have something different happening, instead of the constant tedium of war.

Chapter 13

They rose early the next morning before dawn. After a bountiful breakfast, Caleth, Granthwin, Lunan, and Flioba made ready to depart. To their surprise, Hranthus insisted on coming with them as far as the Jokatone border and offered to let them borrow his horses up until that point. Grateful for his company, and also his protection, they left at once.

After mounting, they departed through a side door, and it wasn't until Caleth looked over his shoulder that he knew why. As he glanced back at the castle, he noticed that there was a camp set up in front of the main gate. Caleth knew at once that it was filled with wizards sent by the Head Caster, and realizing this, he spurred his horse to greater speed. The others followed suit. Luckily, they did not seem to have been noticed, but the party was constantly on its guard.

After a time, they stopped for lunch and reached the border soon after. There, Hranthus bid them farewell and good luck and returned towards his castle with all of his horses.

As they walked into the Endless Plains, the weeds became more unkempt and taller, until they were wading through grass that reached above their knees. It was slow-going and uncomfortable in the hot sun with no shade. Fortunately, Caleth and Flioba could now cast spells, so they summoned a cooling breeze that rushed along the tops of the grasses. However, they could do little about the walking conditions. They did not know the magic word for these tall, annoying plants, and any spell that could cut a path might accidentally set an enormous swathe of the plains ablaze, with them inside it.

After trudging through the endless sea of weeds for many hours, the sun began to set, and they decided to stop for the day. Caleth sank to the ground in despair, his head disappearing beneath the stalks. He thought to himself, "How will we ever get through this?" Sitting forlornly, he let his mind wander. He drifted in and out of consciousness, tired but unwilling to submit to the urge to sleep.

◊◊◊◊◊◊◊

Suddenly, he was looking at himself, although looking was not really the word for it, more like sensing. He saw a clear visual of himself, however, and over to the side were his companions. If this was not odd enough, he seemed to be thinking in a language not his own, a language entirely consisting of magic words, although he could completely understand himself.

After a few minutes, he realized that the thoughts were not his own at all. His mind seemed to have wandered into one of the tall grasses nearby. It took him a while, but eventually he managed to separate his thoughts from those of the plant.

"These humans," the plant thought, "they think they're so high and mighty. They should pay more attention to the world around them. Do they not think they're hurting us when they stomp on us and smash through our homes? How am I to concentrate on growing when these behemoths are about?"

Caleth observed Flioba absentmindedly pulling some of the plants out of the ground and then tossing them to the side.

"That fiend!" the plant exclaimed. "Ripping my comrades up by the roots, eh?! I'd give you a lesson you wouldn't forget, if you'd just come over close enough!"

Without warning, the plant's thoughts changed. Flioba had created another breeze.

"Ah," the plant thought, "that feels so good. I forgive you for your crimes of the past, just keep that breeze flowing. This is wonderful, if only it could go on forever."

Then the thoughts changed again.

"The sun looks bright again today," the plant thought. "It's a good day for growing. Soon I'll make some seeds and raise my own little children. Then they'll grow big and tall."

The plant's thoughts continued on for some time in this sporadic fashion. Caleth delved deeper into the mind, exploring nooks and crannies until he came to the central consciousness of the inner spirit, where the plant's true name was found.

◊◊◊◊◊◊◊

Caleth woke with a start.

"Nelthou!" he shouted.

"What?" asked Granthwin, the closest person to him at the time.

"Nelthou," Caleth repeated. "It's the magic word for the tall grass."

"How'd you happen to find that out?" Flioba inquired, coming over from where Lunan was sitting and then staring at Caleth.

"Well, I'm not sure if you're going to believe this," Caleth replied, "but I think my mind wandered into that of one of the plants. I could listen to its thoughts, and when I wandered around, I found the name. The weirdest part was: it thought in only magic words, but I could understand it since I was inside its mind."

"Hmm," Flioba stated incredulously. "Well, there's only one way to find out."

She began a spell that would dehydrate all of the tall grasses and cause them to droop over until they were no longer as bothersome, but Caleth stopped her.

"Not like that!" Caleth shouted.

"What?" Flioba asked, confused. She stopped the spell.

"When I was inside the plant's mind," Caleth explained, "I learned that plants can feel pain as much as we can. To kill them through dehydration would be cruel. Let me try a different method. I'll use a Reduce spell to temporarily shrink the tall grasses that are near us."

"If you want to…" Flioba said.

Caleth instructed the company to once again gather in a circle with their left hands touching in the middle. Then he drew his rapier and told them to pass it around the group, tracing a circle into the ground around them. As the sword was passed from one to another, Caleth uttered, "*Piklir miri do nelthouix de klion eptona horgak.*" Caleth's sword was passed back to him, and Quazi swelled. He had fully recuperated after fainting at Hranthus' castle. Caleth finished tracing the last arc of the circle, and then all of the tall plants inside the circle shrank to the height of recently mowed grass. Caleth was ecstatic, and Flioba was shocked.

"I guess it did work," Flioba stated.

Lunan laughed at the bitter expression on her face, causing the rest of the company to laugh as well. Then he went to get their packs with all the supplies they had received from Hranthus. As he moved away from the group, he never left the low grass. The tall grass remained the same distance away from him at all times. The rest of the group found that they too could move and take the short grass with them. As soon as they moved, the grass nearest them shrunk and the grass they moved away from grew. It was an unexpected result of the spell, but it pleased the group to no end. This would be the end of their movement problems. From here on out, walking through the Endless Plains would be much easier.

Having created at least a semi-comfortable campsite, Caleth and his friends ate dinner and relaxed for a while. Soon they were feeling drowsy, so they fell asleep just as the stars became visible overhead. They had no idea of the nighttime horrors that awaited them.

Chapter 14

Caleth was rudely awakened by a high pitched shriek. He sat up with a jolt and drew his rapier in a flash, but he did not see the source of the sound. Then he noticed Flioba curled up in a ball next to Lunan. She was whimpering softly.

By now, the rest of their encampment was awake. Everyone looked inquiringly at Flioba, but her eyes were closed and she had started rocking back and forth.

"What is it?" Lunan asked sweetly, as if to a small child who just had a nightmare.

Flioba only pointed a quivering finger in the direction behind them. They turned, and at first could not see anything. But then the moon came out from behind a wispy cloud and with full force shone down upon the ground. What they saw shocked them.

A group of creatures floated eerily above the plains. They were shaped like an oval and were large across the top, but they were exceedingly thin on the sides. Caleth figured this body shape acted like a bag and caught the thermal currents as heat evaporated into the night air.

Their shape, however, was not the strangest part. They were nearly completely transparent, and their organs were easily seen in the light of the moon. Caleth could see a moth struggling to get free from one's stomach. As he watched, it slowly ceased its fight and dissolved, but then another insect appeared in the cavity, coming from a sort of sleeve in the creature's side that must have acted like a mouth. As the creature moved, its body rippled and sometimes it would even completely flip over. Apparently, it didn't matter to the creature which side was up. The moon's light reflected off the creature and made it shine in the night. When Caleth squinted, he could just make out tiny hairs that completely covered its body.

"What is that?" Caleth asked, though he doubted anyone would have the answer.

Surprisingly though, Lunan responded. "It's just a glumfett," he said. "You know; a large, air-dwelling paramecium." Caleth and Granthwin gave him a blank stare. "Forget it, but they're completely harmless."

"Not to moths," Caleth stated.

"Well, no," Lunan responded. "They eat insects, reflecting light from the moon to draw them in, but they never attack humans."

Flioba did not seem reassured. She had stopped shaking, but she was still blubbering on the ground.

"Why are you so upset?" Lunan asked, attempting to calm her.

"W…When I was young," she stammered, "I…I wandered off from my family and…and I got lost. I m…m…must have ended up out here, b…but I didn't know where I was then. I saw one of those…those creatures and it came at m…me with a long whip. I ran b…but I couldn't get away fast enough. It caught up, and it…it beat me." Flioba began to cry again, but after a little while she continued. "I...I lay on the ground in a heap, and eventually it w... went away. I f...finally made it b...back to my village and t...told them what had happened, b...but they didn't believe me. They thought I had just f...fallen into a thorn bush or something. They t...told me to stop lying and were angry at m...me for weeks."

"It's alright," Lunan spoke reassuringly. "These are just glumfetts. The creature that attacked you was probably a snaplora. Did it look like a large peranema?"

"I...I don't know what that is," she replied.

"Oh, right. Sorry," he said. "It looks like the glumfetts, but it also has a long tentacle."

"T...That's what I saw," she responded.

"Well you don't have to worry," Lunan stated. "Glumfetts are docile. This group is wild. Otherwise it would be herded by a snaplora, and there aren't any here."

"I wouldn't be so sure," Caleth said. One of the creatures Lunan had just described had appeared from the opposite side of the glumfetts. It was moving itself towards them using its long tentacle in front to pull it through the air as its body rippled for extra thrust.

Lunan sighed. "Then we will need to kill it," he said. "A snaplora watches out for its herd of glumfetts. It will fight anything and anyone it deems dangerous."

"I'll take care of it," Caleth stated. "You stay with Flioba and make sure she's okay."

Without thinking too much, Caleth cast out his arm towards the snaplora and uttered, "*Konhekto erktox di zargath.*" Unfortunately, he had yawned in the middle, and where he had meant to say 'erkto' he said 'erktox'. The 'x' may not seem like it would have caused any problems, but in the language of magic, an 'x' at the end of a word made it plural. Instead of one arc of fire racing towards the target, five blazing missiles spiraled into the night sky like fireworks, none of them hitting the snaplora.

Put off by his spell's failure, Caleth drew his sword and advanced slowly towards his opponent. He was too tired to think coherently enough to form a spell. He urged Quazi to help fight, but he refused. For some reason, he seemed incapable of attacking anything that was alive.

The glumfetts provided more than enough light to see, even though the snaplora did not reflect any light on its own. The snaplora did not seem to have seen him yet, but then suddenly Caleth had been spotted. It shot forward with extreme speed and lashed out at Caleth, who barely managed to dodge. He stabbed at it as it passed overhead again, and his blade pierced the body of the creature. The snaplora began to lose altitude, but then liquid from its body oozed over the wound and hardened. The creature did not seem to be affected in the least.

"Stabbing it doesn't work!" Lunan shouted. "You have to slash off chunks or it will heal!"

"You couldn't have told me that earlier?!" Caleth shouted back, annoyed.

The snaplora flew at him again; its whip beginning to crack down on his head, but this time Caleth swung his rapier and sliced clean through the tentacle. A high pitched whistling sound rent the air, which Caleth assumed was the creature's scream. Although the whip had been severed from the snaplora's body, the tentacle continued in its motion towards Caleth's face. He attempted to get out of the way, but he was not fast enough. The whip struck him across the cheek, drawing blood, before crashing to the ground and twitching. In a rage, and stricken with pain, the snaplora dropped from the sky toward Caleth's head in an attempt to suffocate him, but before it could land, Caleth slashed in an arc above his head, splitting the creature into two halves, which fell on either side of him.

Unfortunately, this was not the end of his troubles, for the fire show he had accidentally created earlier had drawn other creatures to the area. This time, they were giant mosquitoes, larger than any Caleth had seen before. As they bore down on him, he could see that their probosises were as long as his arm, and sharper than any needle. He stabbed up in desperation, grimacing at the pain from his injury, and his sword found its mark. He had pierced the body of one, and dark blood squirted from the wound onto the ground. Caleth wondered what creature the mosquito had last feasted on. He could not find the strength to raise his rapier again, but luckily for him, the glumfetts had drifted over. Just as one of the mosquitoes went to stab him with its proboscis, a glumfett sucked it into its stomach. The herd made short work of the rest before slowly heading off.

Caleth cried out from the pain of his wound as Lunan ran over to help, leaving Granthwin to comfort Flioba. As Caleth's sight blurred, he saw Lunan preparing some sort of salve, which he rubbed on the injury. Even as Caleth lay there, he felt the salve working. Soon the wound did not hurt, and when Caleth reached his hand up to feel it, he felt only a thin scar.

"How did you do that?" Caleth asked.

"Just snaplora fluid," Lunan replied. "You saw how the creature healed itself. The fluid can help heal a variety of wounds. I'm sure your spells could do it better though."

"No," Caleth responded. "I wouldn't want to risk it without having practiced first. There's no telling what could happen. But I don't understand. How do you know all of this?"

"I just do," Lunan stated. "Do not ask me again. When the time is right, you will know all you need to."

"What's that supposed to mean?!" Caleth exclaimed, confused and angry, but Lunan had already turned and walked back to Flioba. Caleth followed.

"Get some rest," Lunan told him. "I will wake you in a few hours so we can continue on. It would be best for us to travel at night, while we can see the dangers that abound on these plains. We can sleep next when it becomes day. There are fewer troubles then."

Caleth obeyed but was annoyed that Lunan had suddenly gained control of the group. In any case, he did need rest, so he quickly fell into a deep slumber.

◊◊◊◊◊◊◊◊

Before long, Caleth was awakened by Lunan, who wore a troubled expression on his face. When Caleth asked what was wrong, Lunan refused to give a straight answer but insisted they move out at once. In no time, everyone was ready to go, and although tired, they tried their best to remain alert.

Walking about the plains was easy with the spell Caleth had cast the day before. They moved effortlessly, but always watched for creatures that might appear out of the gloom and using the stars to guide them, followed Hranthus' directions to the best of their ability.

For a while, they saw nothing. Then, as they continued walking, they noticed occasional herds of glumfetts, but luckily the creatures were far enough away that they were not any problem. Later on, they observed various other creatures, all odder than the last, and somehow Lunan knew the names of each and the best ways to avoid them. They passed without trouble for the longest time.

Their luck eventually changed, just as night was beginning to give way to the rosy fingers of dawn, they were attacked. A giant worm-like creature reared up out of the grass in front of them and caught them completely by surprise. As if its enormous stature was not enough, the creature was covered with rows of glistening spikes, some coated with blood from its previous victim.

"A giant mosquito larva!" Granthwin exclaimed. "They sometimes cross the border into Quantoff and attack! It took seven warriors once to bring one down!"

They drew their swords and charged the beast, but its hide seemed impenetrable. When they came close, it arched its body and attempted to bite them with its incredibly sharp teeth. Seeing no hope of winning in sight, the company turned to flee, but the larva had coiled its body around them. The spikes made it effectively into a living, barbed wire fence. They were trapped.

The gigantic head of the mosquito larva darted down among the group in an attempt to snatch one of them, but for a time they managed to avoid its efforts. Already exhausted, and their remaining strength waning, it would only be a matter of time before they would become food for the beast. The mosquito snapped down at Caleth, but he managed to jump aside before the jaws tore him asunder. It snaked towards Lunan, but he whapped it on the head with his sword. Everyone seemed to be dodging out of harm's way when the beast struck, until suddenly Granthwin tripped as she leapt clear of the creature's maw.

As the fiendish larva bore down on her, Granthwin was sure she was going to die. She struck with her blade at the sides of its head as she frantically attempted to get out of the way, but her slashes were in vain. When she struck a particularly strong blow, the impact jarred her arm, and she dropped the sword. The rest of the company attacked the beast, stabbing and slashing, but it was no use. The creature went in for the kill, aiming directly at Granthwin's head, but at the last minute, something unbelievable happened. A massive root rose from the ground like an enormous spear and impaled the larva through the mouth as it bore down. The creature's momentum was its downfall. It drove the root deep into its own brain and didn't stop until its head made contact with Granthwin, who was lying beneath it. She was bruised, but alive. The larva did not fare so well. It twitched twice and then collapsed in a lifeless heap. The root fell back to the ground as well and lay motionless. Now the only problem was the recently-living barrier that contained them.

Lunan attempted to climb over the corpse, but the body and spines were covered in some sort of grease that made them exceedingly slippery. After several unsuccessful attempts, they tried hacking at the body with their weapons, but they made little progress. Eventually, Caleth decided that he would have to use a spell. Flioba was too weak to try after her scare earlier that night. They could afford no mistakes. One wrong word could cause any number of problems. After analyzing the risks, Caleth decided that it was not worth it in his tired state. Instead, he proposed that they sleep while safely enclosed, and the others took his suggestion. They could worry about continuing once they were sufficiently rested.

Chapter 15

When Caleth awoke, the sun was high in the sky. Lunan and Flioba were still sleeping, but Granthwin was already up. She was sitting on the ground, staring at where the tremendous root lay. Caleth walked over and sat beside her. She leaned her head on his shoulder, and he placed his arm around her. They remained there silently for a while. Eventually, Granthwin spoke.

"How did it happen?" she asked quietly.

"I don't know," Caleth responded, "but you must have greater magic talents than I ever suspected. What were you thinking at the time?"

"I thought I was going to die," she whispered. "I was scared."

"Perhaps your fear weakened the barriers to your magic. You didn't want to die, so the magic helped, although the root was convenient. There shouldn't be roots out here. Isn't this the Endless Plains?"

Granthwin laughed, a musical sound like that a bird makes on a crisp spring morning. "You must know even less about this area than I do," she said. "Just because it's called the Endless Plains doesn't mean it's just filled with grass. There is the occasional tree and water hole. Weren't you taught anything about geography at that school of yours?"

"Not much," Caleth admitted. "I was only there for one semester." He smiled. "But I've learned more since I've left than even some of the teachers know."

Their conversation was interrupted by snickering coming from behind them. Flioba had just woken up and was smirking at them.

"Having fun?" she asked with a mischievous smile and a raised eyebrow.

"Oh, go summon a chorktol," Caleth said, annoyed.

Granthwin looked at him inquiringly.

"It's a spellcasting saying," Caleth explained. "A chorktol is a bloated, forest-dwelling creature that floats because the gases inside of it are lighter than air. It moves around by expelling these fumes. A really unpleasant creature to be sure, not to mention it smells like rotten eggs."

"I see," Granthwin replied.

She got to her feet, and Caleth reluctantly did the same. He sighed, not knowing when their next peaceful moment together might be. While he was lost in his thoughts, Flioba woke Lunan, who leapt to his feet in a flash.

"Well," he said, "are you going to take care of this problem?"

"One moment, one moment," Caleth responded. "Flioba, you're sure you don't want to do it?"

"I think I'll save my energy," she said, as if her ability to cast spells was more important than Caleth's. "You go ahead."

Caleth scowled. "Alright," he said, "here goes."

He had decided on using ice and air magic so as to eliminate most risks, like creating a barrier of fire or something. He made sure Quazi was ready before starting. Then he reached out to touch the slimy body while uttering, *"Ikanjau futax de hre grefa, keol ikanjau kutax pluno."* The corpse grew colder and colder until it was like a solid block of ice. Caleth withdrew his hand.

Then he began to cast a spell which would smash the frozen creature. *"Konhekto panthuerno ji draktoneth masu kua huilon kuta tiro kua piktol kol grefa,"* he intoned, pointing to the body. A breeze began to flow in the direction of his arm, and the company felt it gain in strength. Suddenly, it became almost visible, like a solid chunk of air, and smashed into the frozen body. Being brittle, the ice exploded into hundreds of pieces, leaving only the spines intact and scattered across the grass. There was now a hole in their enclosure.

Caleth collapsed from the strain of casting two powerful spells, one right after the other, but Granthwin caught him before he hit the ground. They waited a few minutes for him to regain his strength before leaving the relative safety the barrier had ensured. Before they had completely left the area, Lunan remembered something.

"Wait," he said. "We should take the spines that are now disconnected from the creature. They can fetch an enormous sum at market."

Taking his advice, they gathered up the spines that lay littered across the ground. They left the rest on the larva's body since they had no good way to remove them. With this done, they decided to follow the root to its source. The sun was beating down hard on their backs, and any amount of shade would feel wonderful, even for a bit.

The root was long, but soon they could see the top of an enormous tree in the distance. It was not exceedingly tall, but the trunk was as wide as an entire village and the canopy of leaves extended over a vast area. As they got closer, they could see that the tree was on the edge of a tiny pond, which was surrounded by low-lying bushes. Cattails rose from the middle of the water, which looked like it should be frequented by thirsty animals. However, at the moment, none were there. Although this might seem odd, the group took little notice. They were too excited that they would soon be able to refill their canteens and rest away from the sun's hot gaze.

The prospect of water and shade drew the company closer, but before they arrived at their destination, they noticed that there were living creatures beneath the tree. In fact, they were men. These men were fully clothed in silk, and not even their faces were visible beneath silk hoods. The instant Lunan saw them, he recoiled with a look of fear in his eyes.

"What is it?" Caleth asked. "Do you know these men?"

"In a way," Lunan responded. "That group is a nezlon. We need to back away."

He walked away from the tree, and the others followed, confused.

"What's a nezlon?" Flioba asked.

"A group of assassins that work together to kill one person," Lunan replied. "I guess I have to tell you everything. I really wanted to avoid this, but I guess I have no choice."

"Tell us what?" Flioba inquired, frowning.

"I was not born a Quantoffan," Lunan stated. "In fact, I was not born anywhere in your known world. Jokatone and Quantoff are not the only places humans inhabit on this planet. There is a land far out on the Endless Plains. It was built along the river Yanfall. That is where I am from."

"What do you mean?" Caleth asked.

"Let me finish," Lunan said, "before I decide that telling you is a bad idea."

Caleth shut his mouth and listened.

"The land along the Yanfall River is known as Holtony. It is not at war with anyone, and has remained at peace for a long time. Being at peace has allowed its inhabitants time to become more technologically advanced than your people. Sure, your magic can accomplish the same things as our technology, but we have no magic. Although we have the same capabilities some of the time, we have used our technology to learn about the world around us, instead of to continually help us kill.

"However, that does not mean there is no violence in our land. There certainly is. We may not fight a continual war, but there are assassins who will do you in while you sleep if you have made a powerful enough enemy. From a young age, I was trained to be a ranger assassin. I was taught how to survive in the wilderness, which for us just meant the plains, and I learned about many of the creatures that dwell near our lands, both big and small. This is how I know all of that information about the glumfetts and other creatures we have seen. The reason I was taught this information was to be a more effective killer, and to be able to pursue my target even if he ran. For a while, I was fine with this. It paid well, and I rationalized my killings so that they did not seem as bad.

"This all changed when I was given a contract to assassinate a young child. I did not know why he was targeted to be killed, and we did not ask questions. It was a job, no more. I had my doubts about being able to kill the boy, and when I saw him, looking as innocent as could be, I could not do it. There was no way I could kill him. That being the case, I fled.

"I didn't know where to go, and I was scared. I knew they would send a nezlon after me since no contract can be walked out on without consequences ensuing. My superiors would want me dead for disobeying. I didn't know that there were other people in other lands, and I stumbled onto yours by mistake. I suspect that there are those among my people who do know of your kingdoms, but they won't tell the masses because they don't want Holtony to be sucked into any conflict.

"Regardless, I ended up in Quantoff and signed myself up to join the army, since all I knew how to do was kill. I quickly moved up in rank due to skills I had developed as an assassin. My success as a swordsmaster did not ease my mind. I always have known that I would some day have to face a nezlon and revisit old memories best left undisturbed. You know the rest from there."

"Wow," said Caleth, "that is quite a tale." His mind was spinning from the implications of what Lunan had told them. There was so much he had not been taught in school.

"We should be moving on," Lunan stated. "We have wasted too much time already. We must hurry and hope we are not spotted. Defeating a nezlon in battle is not an easy trick, and one rarely lets a battle break out. Assassins prefer to kill when the target is unaware of them."

They quickly, but reluctantly, walked away from the tree, continually looking over their shoulder in fear of an attack, but none came. They were disappointed that they would not be able to rest in the shade and replenish their water supply, but there was little they could do. Luckily, they did not need to refill their canteens at the pond since they could obtain water magically, but it never tasted as good.

Soon they were well away from the area, and once they thought they were no longer in danger, they rested. Once night fell, they would need to continue, but for now they could afford to sleep. Just in case, though, Flioba cast a Concealment spell over their campsite so that it would be undetectable.

Chapter 16

A week went by without trouble. The group kept checking for pursuit, but as far as they could tell, they were not being followed. Throughout this time, Lunan served as their guide and helped them navigate the terrain without difficulty. No creatures attacked, but they saw a fair number along the way that slinked off into the night when the company drew near.

By now they had arrived at a small, rocky area. Pillars of stone taller than a man reached up towards the clouds as if in defiance of some unknown act. In the night, they looked eerily reminiscent of the teeth of some great beast. Lunan stopped here for a moment and turned to his companions.

"I crossed through here when I left my homeland," he stated. "We are close to the Quantoff border."

Excited at the prospect of escaping potential terrors in the Endless Plains, the company hurried off after Lunan towards Quantoff, and human habitation. Soon they would be among other people again, though whether that was a good thing was yet to be determined. One thing was sure, though: they couldn't let on that Caleth and Flioba were Jokatonans. Magic would also be a bad idea, at least when among other humans. They would probably be safe using spells along empty roads while they travelled, though having Quazi out might look suspicious.

Before long, they left the tall grasses of the Plains behind them and entered the more tame terrain of Quantoff. The native animals and insects here were a normal size and definitely less threatening. The company walked through a grassy field, and they soon came to a small wooded area on the edge of a dirt road. Here they stopped for a brief respite that extended into a prolonged rest. They decided it would be best to sleep until the middle of the day so as not to startle anyone they came upon, and could finally go back to sleeping at night and travelling during the day, instead of the other way around.

◊◊◊◊◊◊◊

They woke to a warm breeze caressing their faces. After a skimpy breakfast, the group prepared to head out. Before they could travel any farther into Quantoff lands, they had to decide on a back story. If the group were questioned, as they most likely would be, they needed to have matching answers since they were all of the age where they should have been in the army.

"We will have to include the army somewhere in our story," Lunan stated. He had been in the army longer than the rest of them and so knew more about its inner workings. "Maybe we can say we are a specialized unit. They have those, you know. They're assigned missions that can be handled by a small group of highly trained fighters. We'd just have to think of a mission."

"We'd need a unit name too," Caleth put in.

"How about the 'Fighting Furies'?" Flioba offered.

"The 'Death Drinkers'?" Lunan suggested.

"The 'Slashing Slayers' or the 'Titan Tippers'?" Granthwin offered.

"The 'Fighting Furies' sounds good," Caleth stated.

The rest of the group agreed, but Lunan did only reluctantly. He still liked the 'Death Drinkers'.

"Now we just need a mission," Flioba stated.

"Well, what's far to the south of Quantoff?" Caleth asked.

"Uh, the hills at the base of the Shield Mountains," Granthwin replied. "Sometimes a swarm of ratches comes from there into Quantoff. Maybe we could say we were sent to take care of one?"

Caleth knew from battle school that a ratch was a small, bloodsucking creature that could travel at great speeds along the ground. One was virtually harmless and easily killed, but a swarm could overrun a group of people or even an entire village, leaving nothing but desiccated corpses.

"Works for me," Caleth stated.

"Yes," Lunan said, "I think that will do just fine."

After a short time longer going over details, until they were sure they had their back story straight, the company left their campsite from the night before and set off south down the dirt road. In high spirits, the group did not look back, though later they realized that this was a big mistake.

◊◊◊◊◊◊◊

The road was not much travelled, since most people were either in the army up north or content to stay within the confines of their villages. Occasionally a merchant would pass by, attempting to peddle his wares to anyone he could find. The Fighting Furies didn't buy anything, though, since they had little money and didn't want to reveal that they possessed giant mosquito larva spines, which might tempt people into thievery.

The company was not questioned by ordinary travelers and traders, who thought their business was their own, but occasionally a small squadron of troops would pass by with the leader demanding information. Luckily they were able to avoid any larger troop movements by ducking off of the path when they heard a loud din coming towards them. If a large body of soldiers saw them, their leader would probably be a high enough rank to know to demand papers to verify their information, papers which Caleth and his companions did not possess. The squadron leaders, on the other hand, were newly promoted and knew little of the military knowledge common to those with experience. They bought the Fighting Furies' story and even gave the group some of their food to help them on their way. The army protected its own.

On their tenth day in Quantoff, Granthwin alerted them to the fact that they were approaching the town of her birth, Fadrinley. She seemed excited to see her family again, but for some reason she was also a little reserved. She told them that the people who went to The Steel Mule were not exactly of high caliber, and that they should be very careful not to insult anyone in any way, since fights often broke out with little warning.

Fadrinley was not a large town, consisting of a spattering of houses with a small marketplace in the center, around which a few shops were located. The Steel Mule was on the western edge of the marketplace, just behind the food stands. It was a wooden, two-story building painted green, with windows situated in a symmetrical manner. Over the entryway, which had seen better days, a sign was hanging consisting of a picture of an armored mule, its face watching the people who entered, and the words 'The Steel Mule' painted above the animal in a semi-circle.

Granthwin sighed upon seeing the sign and braced herself a moment before pushing the door open and stepping inside with her companions behind her. The interior was bustling with activity since they had arrived just before evening and the tavern was beginning to fill up. As they walked over to an empty table, everyone on either side seemed to recognize Granthwin. Some reached out to touch her, drunk, but she slapped their hands away. After they had seated themselves, one of the barmaids noticed Granthwin and came right over.

"Granthwin, is that really you, sweetie?" she asked in an amazingly maternal voice for someone who appeared so gruff.

"Mother," Granthwin replied, smiling. "It's so good to see you again."

"You too, darling; and who are your friends?"

"Caleth, Lunan, and Flioba," Granthwin informed her, pointing to each person as she gave the names.

"Good, good. You are all very welcome to stay here. Any friend of our Granthwin is a friend of ours."

"Thank you," they responded.

"You are very generous," Caleth stated.

"Oh, think nothing of it," Granthwin's mother replied. She turned back to Granthwin. "Wait just one minute and I'll get your father. He'll be very happy to see you."

However, when Granthwin's father was dragged over to the table by her mother, he looked anything but happy to see her.

"What are you doing here?" he asked in a voice hoarse from shouting over the din of his tavern. "You're supposed to be in the army!" He glared sternly at her. Here, Caleth thought, was the Steel Mule himself.

"I am, Father," she replied. "I was chosen to be part of a specialized unit, the Fighting Furies. These people here are the rest of that unit."

"That's real good," her father said, beaming. "I'm impressed. But," he said, still suspicious, "what are you doing as far south as this?"

"We were ordered to take care of a swarm of ratches," she answered. "Particularly nasty bunch, I'm told."

"I haven't heard about any," her father stated, doubtful for some reason that she was telling the truth.

"The army hasn't let the information out to the public," she said, spinning lies as she went. "It doesn't want the people nearby to panic, so don't spread the information around. However, they needn't fear now that we've come."

"You really think you can take care of a swarm of ratches?" he asked, cynical as always.

"You haven't seen us fight," she stated.

"Well there'll be no fighting here," he stated sternly. "And as long as you're here, you need to work."

"But…" Granthwin started.

"No buts," her father stated. "You're my daughter, and you'll do what I say."

Granthwin's mother tried to reason with him, but it was no use. It seemed once he made up his mind, there was no way to change it.

Just as Granthwin stood up in a huff, the clang of a crossbow bolt on steel rang out. The noise in the tavern quieted into silence as the people looked around for where the sound had come. Caleth turned towards Lunan and saw that he had drawn his blade, the crossbow bolt lying on the floor beside him, smeared with a greenish substance. Apparently Lunan's years of training to be a ranger assassin had allowed him to hear the twang of the crossbow as it released its missile, and he had instinctually drawn his sword.

Granthwin's father looked up to see where the bolt had come

from, and Caleth did the same. He hadn't noticed before that the second level was open in the center with a balcony around the edge and rooms off of that. Six men crouched along the edge of the balcony. It was the nezlon.

Seeing the men, Granthwin's father shouted a war cry and ran up the stairs, ready to kill them with his bare hands. As he ran, Lunan yelled out a warning.

"Be careful, the bolts are poisoned!" he shouted.

Caleth, Granthwin, and Flioba rose to stand with Lunan and each drew their blade. They could not use magic here amongst so many Quantoffans. Several more bolts were fired. They managed to dodge two, and Flioba was able to block another with her longsword. The rapiers Caleth and Flioba used were too narrow to block a bolt. In this chaos, the other patrons fled the tavern, leaving it empty except for the Fighting Furies and Granthwin's mother and father.

By the time Granthwin's father had reached the balcony, the assassins had hurled themselves over, landing nimbly on their feet and drawing their daggers, which also were coated in the green poison. Seeing the assassins so easily make the jump, Granthwin's father also leapt down, landing heavily on a table and smashing it with his fall. Having hurt his legs, he spent a long time attempting to extricate himself from the rubble.

The assassins took no notice of him, though. The nezlon instead surrounded Lunan and his friends, forcing them to form a defensive circle, back to back. The assassins advanced steadily, until the only barrier between them and their prey was the Fighting Furies' swords. These, Lunan and the others used to great success. Lunan had not been promoted to Minor Swordsmaster for nothing, and Caleth and Granthwin fought as a team.

The assassins must have been startled by their skill, since two lost their daggers in their first clash with their opponents' swords. As they fought, the Fighting Furies were unnerved by the grim determination of the assassins, who showed no emotion even when injured. It was a difficult and harsh battle, but eventually the assassins were overwhelmed by the skill of the Fighting Furies, and the length of their swords. Before long, they were defeated, though apparently they were not all quite dead.

Seeing that the assassins were presumably killed, Granthwin's mother rushed over to her husband from across the room. Unfortunately for her, she came between one of the assassins and Lunan. Attempting to kill his target with a surprise attack, one of the assassins had played dead and launched his dagger towards Lunan. The assassin must not have expected Granthwin's mother to race across the room when the dagger impaled her in the side. Granthwin shrieked and charged the assassin, sticking him with her sword over and over. Eventually, Caleth pulled her away, while her mother lay on the floor twitching.

Granthwin's father finally managed to pull himself out of the wreckage of the table and crawled towards his wife. Granthwin fell weeping next to her. Caleth tried to comfort her, but he doubted he succeeded. Flioba seemed on the verge of tears herself. Only Lunan remained calm and took control of the situation.

The poison was fast-acting. Granthwin's mother had already fallen unconscious and even her twitching had slowed. Lunan knelt down next to her and pulled the dagger from her side. He then began sucking the poison from her wound and spitting it onto the floor.

"What are you doing to my wife?!" Granthwin's father exclaimed.

"Please, sir," Lunan responded calmly, "I'm just attempting to extract the poison, if you'll let me. If you value your wife's life, please get me a grapefruit."

"A grapefruit!?" Granthwin's father shouted. "My wife's dying, and you're going to eat a grapefruit?! Do you know how hard one is to find?!"

"It's not for me," Lunan explained. "Grapefruit juice can be used as an antidote for this poison."

Granthwin's father mellowed slightly. "Are you sure?" he asked.

"Quite," Lunan replied. "Now hurry, she doesn't have much time."

Granthwin's father raced limping out of the building with a look of savage determination. Within minutes, he was back.

"I found one right outside," he spoke breathlessly as he handed Lunan the grapefruit.

Lunan quickly sliced the fruit in half with his sword and squeezed the juice from one half into the wound. The juice from the other half he squeezed into her mouth and made her swallow. He waited several minutes and then checked her pulse.

"She'll be alright," he said to the relief of Granthwin and her father.

"Do you know how much that fruit cost?!" Granthwin's father shouted. "It's not easy getting those things to grow around here, and I didn't even have time to haggle over the price!"

"Here is something for your troubles," Caleth said as he handed him one of the giant mosquito larva spines. "We are very sorry to have caused harm to befall you and your wife."

Granthwin's father took the offering but still he was angry. "You nearly killed my wife!" he exclaimed. "And you put my daughter in harm's way! I want the lot of you out of here."

"But father…" Granthwin pleaded.

"All right, dear," he replied, "I guess you're right. You did manage to salvage the situation, and you say my wife will be fine. I'll let you stay one night, but no more. In the meantime, I'll have to sell this spine and use the money I get for it to attract back the customers you've lost me, not to mention replace this table."

Although word of the evening's events had already spread throughout the town, a few people did still come into the tavern, if only to see the wreckage. The assassins' bodies were disposed of, and the Fighting Furies were able to sleep for one night in regular beds. The situation was not nearly as dire as it had seemed, and Granthwin's mother eventually woke and resumed her usual duties. If nothing else, at least they no longer had to worry about being followed. Lunan assured them that a nezlon always consisted of six and no more. For now, they were safe.

Chapter 17

When they woke, the group was happily surprised to find full packs waiting for them. After the occurrences of the night before, they had been unsure if they would receive any help from Granthwin's family. Granthwin's father was not quite as angry as the night before, but he was still as gruff as usual.

The Fighting Furies ate a good breakfast and set out as soon as possible. Granthwin hung back a moment to say goodbye to her parents but soon joined with the others, ready to leave. They departed at once, happy with the weight of their newly-filled packs.

Before long, they reached the southern border of Quantoff, marked by the beginning of rolling hills, extending out to mountains on the horizon. Caleth sighed, knowing that this would be a more strenuous part of their journey. Without comment, each one hefted their packs and strode on.

It was the second day when trouble struck. The company had just crested a ridge and was surveying the land beyond it, when

Flioba suddenly pointed out something odd beneath them.

"What's that?" she asked, gesturing towards a section of the landscape where the ground itself appeared to be moving towards them.

"I don't know," Lunan replied. "I'm not very familiar with this terrain."

"Wait," said Granthwin, "I think those are ratches!"

And so they were. When Caleth looked closer, he could make out individual creatures amid the swarm. The creatures looked like oversized ticks, but they were moving fast, too fast, faster than seemed possible.

"They'll be on us in less than a minute," he stated breathlessly.

"Quick, let's hide in there," Lunan suggested, pointing towards a small alcove amid a pile of rocks.

"No," Granthwin said firmly. "They are heading towards Quantoff. Our story was true. The town I grew up in lies directly in their path. They'll kill everyone; my parents will be dead! We have to stop them!"

"But how?" Lunan asked. "There are too many, even if we managed to fend them off for a while, they would undoubtedly overrun us eventually."

"I have an idea," Caleth stated. "Flioba, you and I will rain fire down upon them. Follow my lead. Lunan and Granthwin, we will need you both to cover us and kill any of the ratches that make it through our bombardment. Sound like a plan?"

Caleth's companions agreed, and everyone quickly took their posts. Lunan and Granthwin drew their swords and stood at the ready. Caleth began to pick rocks off the ground and put them in his left hand. When he ran out of rocks, he squeezed dirt into chunks. Flioba did the same as Caleth, but did not yet understand where he was going with it. As the front of the swarm reached the base of the hill where they stood, Caleth acted.

"*Zargoth!*" he yelled and threw one of the rocks. Then he took another with his right hand and threw it, yelling the same word. Flioba began imitating him. As the rocks left their hands, they burst into flame and fell upon the ratches below. Either because of the eternal fire gem Caleth wore or the influence of Quazi, Caleth's rocks exploded when they hit the ground, blasting a hole where ratches had been. Anyone watching would have been able to tell whose missiles were whose based on their appearance as they fell down into the swarm. Flioba's left a fiery streak in the air as they went, while Caleth's sparked across the sky. These flaming missiles caused massive devastation to the ratches, but once they had seen the group of humans, became focused solely on feeding off of them, no matter the cost.

"*Zargoth!*" A group of ratches exploded, setting several others alight. "*Zargoth!*" A cluster went up in flame. "*Zargoth!*" Destruction rained down upon the ratches but still they came. The burning ratches let out high-pitched wails before popping with a bang. Dead bodies littered the ground. The first ratches reached the crest of the hill and lunged at Lunan and Granthwin, who managed to slash and skewer them. "*Zargoth!*" Flames erupted on the far side of the swarm, causing more screaming. "*Zargoth!*" Streaks of fire lit the air, and sparks showered the ratches below. More and more were reaching the company. Lunan and Grathwin were fending them off, but some got through and had to be yanked off the skin before they fully attached. "*Zargoth!*" Caleth threw a close one, and Lunan wiped ratch guts off his face. "*Zargoth!*" Flioba aimed for the center, attempting to scatter the ratches so they came in more of a line and less of a swarm. "*Zargoth!*" Massive explosions shook the ground. Caleth had thrown the rest of his rocks and dirt all at once in an arc across the field. He spared a moment to grab whatever he could off the ground for use as more missiles. "*Zargoth!*" A ratch had lunged for Lunan's head, but Flioba's missile smashed it out of the air. Hope entered their hearts as they saw that the swarm was thinning.

In the end, they managed to kill all the ratches, but at quite a price. Caleth and Flioba had used too much magic in one day, and lay nearly unconscious on the ground. Without rest, they would be completely helpless. Lunan and Granthwin had the worst physical damage, wounds from where stray ratches had gotten through their defenses. Lunan applied snaplora fluid to their wounds, and to the few that Caleth and Flioba had as well. They could go no farther at the moment.

◊◊◊◊◊◊◊

It took two days for the company to fully recover. Although sore, they could finally move on. Three days later they reached the mountains, their tall crags reaching for the sky. Although the tops were rocky, the bases of the mountains were covered in trees. The peaks were difficult to cross, with steep climbs and narrow ledges along with occasional slippery descents. One wrong step could cause a tremendous fall and often death. The mountain air was cooler than in the hills, and the company put on warmer clothing from their supplies. The mountains seemed to stretch forever, but still they trekked on.

On their third day in the mountains, they came to a spot near the top of one peak that was devoid of trees. From there, the group could see far out into the distance. In front of them was a valley, surrounded by mountains on all sides and containing an enormous lake, bigger than any they had seen before. On the side of the lake facing them there seemed to be some sort of town, except that it was a lot bigger than any ordinary town. It seemed to have once held a vast number of people, but now the buildings laid in ruin. The oddest part about the town was that the buildings were not made out of standard building materials such as wood and stone. Instead, they were built of metal. The entire place seemed to be filled with things made of metal. Another interesting feature was a large scorch mark, barely visible across most of the town. As far as everyone could tell, no one was still living there. They wondered who had constructed such odd buildings and contraptions, but they had no answers.

Looking towards the southwest, they could just make out an enormous mountain, taller than all the others and capped with snow on its peak. Knowing this was where they were heading, the quartet was still unsure of what would happen when they met the dragon, if it still lived there at all.

Gazing out over a vast area, Caleth couldn't help wondering how the mountains got their name. Who were the Shield Mountains protecting, and from what? These were just more questions that would probably never be resolved.

◊◊◊◊◊◊◊

Getting to the snow-capped peak was not easy; the journey was long and treacherous. After travelling for many days, they finally reached their destination. In front of them lay an enormous mountain, larger than any they had climbed thus far. Now they only needed to find the cave where the dragon dwelt.

Before continuing, though, each one stopped to remind themselves of what Hranthus had told them. The dragon did not want to be called a 'dragon'. Instead, it wanted to be called a 'vashaka'. Also, the dragon's name was Marinteya the All-Knowing, and it had a falling-out with humans long ago. They would have to be careful in what they said and how they acted.

Finding the cave was an arduous task. Not only was the mountain immense, but it was also covered in dense foliage. Finding a cave, even a large one, was nearly impossible. However, after many long hours of searching, they eventually discovered it, nearly hidden from view behind large trees and vines, causing it to blend into the surroundings.

Without knowing exactly what to expect, the company ventured forth into the cave, if it could even be called a cave; consisting of many rooms and passages, it might best have been termed a tunnel complex. The outer layers looked just as a cave or tunnel should: rock, wet at times, with occasional stalactites and stalagmites. Deeper into the cave they encountered a few gold coins, and later on more treasures and riches. The closer they got to the heart of the mountain, the more the piles of valuables increased. In further corridors and rooms, shelves ran alongside the riches, stuffed full of books with not a spot left empty. The oddest thing about the tunnel complex was that it was completely devoid of life. Not one bat hung from the ceiling, and there were no subterranean mosses or fungi. They passed through many tunnels, somewhat in fear of what was to come, but this fear was overshadowed by the growing wonder of what they saw.

Glancing at the book covers, Caleth realized that he knew hardly any of the languages in which they were written. Some were in the common tongue, others obviously in the language of magic, and some, Caleth thought, looked like they might be written in kralthak. These were the only ones he recognized. The rest consisted of a variety of different looking languages, many of which did not even use the same alphabet as the common tongue. Where did these all come from? Caleth knew of no lands where they might have originated, he had only been taught the geography of his small world: Jokatone and Quantoff.

After countless dead ends and other obstacles, the company eventually reached the heart of the mountain. How they knew it was the heart, they could not say, but they knew it all the same. They stood in a massive chamber, filled with gold and other riches. On the walls and in neat stacks lay innumerable books, and among the other valuables lay old maps, some only partially complete and most depicting areas unknown to the group. It was in this room that they had expected to encounter the dragon, but the only form of life other than themselves was a small beetle crawling across a mound of gold coins.

The company was frustrated with their lack of success, but they still felt that the dragon was hiding in the tunnel complex somewhere.

"Marinteya is probably watching us right now," Caleth stated.

Flioba let loose an outburst of anger. "All of this and all we find is a stupid beetle?!" she exclaimed and went to crush the beetle under her foot.

"Wait," Lunan said, attempting to stop her, "she may still be here. There is no reason to kill an innocent beetle."

However, he could not stop her in time. As her foot bore down on the beetle, the insect suddenly changed. Its figure momentarily blurred before an immense golden dragon glared down at them, its wings unfurling to their fullest extent as a rooster does when it attempts to intimidate a threat. With this change, there were little of the showy qualities of Hranthus' metamorphosis.

The dragon snarled at them and its forked tongue darted out of its mouth. Then it hissed and began bobbing its neck up and down like an angry goose. The Fighting Furies cowered in fear, unsure of whether to run. The dragon did not advance, and Caleth finally spoke.

"Marinteya the All-Knowing, I presume," he stated in an

attempt at sounding bold and unafraid, though what came out was more of a squeak.

"Vua kol lajas huilon, ji vua kuar lajas prodo kro?" Marinteya replied, then seeing they did not understand, asked again in the common tongue. "Who are you, and why have you come?"

"We were told by Hranthus that you could grant us a favor," Caleth stated, "but we do not come asking a favor for nothing." He had thought of this idea after seeing the mounds of treasure throughout the tunnel complex. Never taking his eyes off the dragon, he retrieved the remaining giant mosquito spines and laid them in front of Marinteya. "A gift for you," he said.

"Ah, Hranthus," Marinteya said, relaxing slightly, "quite a young one of our kind. Unfortunately, the young are ignorant of their history. They think they are the 'dragons' that men named them."

"We were told you were a vashaka," Caleth stated.

"Really?" Marinteya asked. "Hranthus told you this?"

"Yes," Caleth replied.

"Perhaps the young do retain some knowledge of ages past," Marinteya remarked.

She had stopped bobbing her head and now sat on her haunches in front of them. She no longer looked as menacing. Marinteya sighed, and then her body began to blur again, and when the metamorphosis was complete, the company was staring at a kralthak.

"Marinteya?" Caleth asked, confused.

"We were all kralthaks originally," she told him. "The young were so taken by their 'dragon' form that they eventually forgot they were actually not huge, winged reptiles and were in fact kralthaks. It is a pity really, such a loss of knowledge through the ages."

"Just a question," Caleth said.

"Yes?"

"Were you speaking in the language of magic when you originally spoke to us?"

"Yes, as you call it," she replied. "In ancient times, all living things spoke the same language: the language of magic as you call it now. We just called it the Language."

"How are you not casting a spell when you speak it?" Caleth asked. He had been wondering this for some time, ever since he had wandered into the mind of the tall grass and it had thought solely in the language of magic.

"There is a difference in the mind between speaking and spellcasting, a different way of thinking," she answered. "But you still haven't told me who you are?"

"I am Caleth Rictanson, Kralthak-Saver," he told her, "and these are Granthwin Molgonsdatter, Lunan Pertwitson, and Flioba Tradbensdatter."

"Kralthak-Saver, eh?" Marinteya remarked. "Who did you save?"

"The Great Lord Thowgotel Filfwanderson," Caleth replied.

"I have not heard of him," she responded, "but his father is known to me. He is the best King he thinks he can be, though he should lead his people out of the Desolate Fields. An existence there can hardly be called an existence at all. Now, what is this favor you would have of me?"

"Granthwin has strong magical potential as I'm sure you can sense," Caleth stated, "but she has not been Awakened, and as she is not from Jokatone, the Jokatone spellcasters will not Awaken her. Can you do it?"

"The last time I Awakened a human," Marinteya said, "everything went wrong. Humans became an unstoppable, invasive species, destroying many of the native species that lived here. Let me tell you a little of your own history, history that your own race has forgotten."

Chapter 18

"Long before humans first appeared, kralthaks roamed this world. They were the undisputed masters of their domain, but they were kind and gentle to those beneath them. In those days, everything spoke the Language; even the plants could speak out loud so that others could hear. Seeing as the kralthaks could hear how every living thing fared, they were able to take each organism's views into account and govern justly.

Within these kralthaks, there was a special group, separated from the others by an ability perhaps brought about through a genetic mutation, to change form. These shapeshifters were called vashakax. Most of the time, the vashakax stayed in their kralthak forms, but when frightened, they often changed into a monstrous, winged reptile, a form created in order to intimidate potential enemies.

During this ancient time, I was a youth, minding my own business away from other kralthaks, as vashakax often did. I lived near a lake that was enclosed by mountains. Perhaps you saw it on your journey here. It was called Arlag do Jika, which is translated into the common tongue as the Lake of Life. There I lived, content to spend my days fishing and eating my catch.

However, one day something unusual occurred. Bodies were floating up to the surface of the lake, and not just any bodies, bodies of a creature I had never encountered before. These creatures seemed to be around the same size as a kralthak, but they had little hair in comparison and no tail to speak of. The clothes they wore were foreign and strange. These were the first humans on this world, but certainly not the last.

In fright, I changed into the winged lizard and flew away from the area. I knew not where to go or what to do, so I stayed around, watching, always watching. For a long time I stayed away from the lake, occasionally surveying the area to see what was happening.

Although at first the humans were drowning, some eventually made it to the surface alive, and when they did, they began doing strange things. They talked to themselves, and I figured they were probably crazy. This feeling was reaffirmed when they began bringing metals to the edge of the lake from their underwater lair. They at first built a small shack, large enough only to house the men when they slept, and then they built an odd contraption. It looked like an enormous pillar on its side with a rounded tip, and large blades were placed on the back, probably, I thought, to fight off threats. To my amazement, the men sent it back underwater, with some inside.

Once this contraption had been sent back beneath the lake, more and more people began arriving. Soon there were more people in one place than in the largest group of kralthaks I had ever seen. They were like ants, always industrious and always pouring from beneath the water like from a newly opened ant hole. There seemed to be no end to their arrivals, and once they came, they built lodgings, bigger and bigger lodgings, larger than any I had seen before. They also created various other devices, the functions of which I did not know.

I was curious. These creatures were like none I had ever seen before. How did they come from the water and yet drown in it? They were a mystery to me, and I wanted to find out who they were and where they came from. In order to accomplish this end, I transformed myself into a fish, a small one so I would not be noticed, and dove deep beneath the water.

The bottom of the lake was riddled with tunnels and caves, and it took me a long time to find where the men originated. I tried to stay away from the metal pillar so that I would not be attacked, but eventually I had to follow it in order to discover where it went.

The metal pillar stopped in one dead end. As I gazed into the tunnel, I was surprised to see humans appearing where a small machine had been left on the ground, apparently by the first person to appear. This machine created some kind of portal, which filled the entire end of the tunnel from floor to ceiling. It shimmered with a light that did not come from the sun at the surface.

As I watched, a woman emerged from the portal and swam a short distance to the metal pillar. A hatch opened for her, and she passed through some material that held the water back but let her pass through. I had never seen anything like it before. Then the hatch closed, and the metal pillar propelled itself back to the surface to drop the woman off before returning to wait for more people.

I was scared of these creatures with their metal constructions, but also intrigued. I returned to the surface and decided to make contact with the humans, but just to be safe I changed into my winged lizard form so I could attack or flee if necessary.

When I approached the humans, they were frightened. They

shouted the word 'dragon' over and over again and quickly ran for weapons. They began to fire at me with metal sticks, and hot lead shot through the air near my head. I pleaded with them to stop, and one must have realized I was trying to communicate because he forced the others to end their attack.

They then brought out a machine that they probably used to translate languages, but it did not seem to work. I do not know why it didn't work, but I assume it was something to do with the magical nature of the Language. Realizing they were at least trying to converse with me, I cast a quick translating spell, allowing them to hear the Language as they would their own, and allowing me to understand their speech.

I angrily told them that they had taken my home, and they apologized. However, they said they could not move at this point and that I would have to live near another part of the lake. This angered me, but I realized I could do little about it. At least if they knew where I was living, I thought, they might not bother me again.

I asked them where they came from, but they did not give any answer I understood, something about coming from another world. I guess they meant a region like the Plane of Elementals, a place that you could connect to via portals. Eventually, I found out that they were investigating potential places for their expansion. I was disturbed at the thought of metal fortresses throughout my lands, and I thought more than once of killing or driving them off before they could make much progress. However, I decided it would be best to befriend them instead of making a dangerous enemy.

In peace, I withdrew to think. For a while, I continued to watch over the humans, making sure they were not doing anything malevolent. During this time, they began to bring me precious metals, for some reason thinking that I required them. Although this was untrue, possibly a fact about the "dragons" of which they had spoken before, I let them continue because I didn't mind increasing my wealth. Who would refuse gifts of riches?

Later on, I saw a group of humans leaving to colonize near the ocean. When I asked about it, the men said they needed a stable supply of food, and fishing was often an easy way to obtain it. Apparently there weren't enough fish in the lake to support them all.

I let the men settle by the ocean because they had a valid reason for it, but soon other humans wanted to colonize different regions of the world. I did not want this to happen, but it seemed I could do little. Before I let them settle throughout the lands, I forced them to agree to governance by vashakax. In this way, the original inhabitants of the world would still have the most control of it.

As a token of friendship, I gave one man the greatest gift I could. His name was Parlo, and I had thought he was a good man. Unfortunately, even good men can create bad situations. I Awakened Parlo and taught him an Awakening spell. With this knowledge, I had thought humans would be more in tune with the planet. I was mistaken.

Some were fine, I'll admit, but others could not handle their newfound power. A few went crazy, casting spells left and right without regard to the consequences. Blinded with power, some of the men drove me to a cave in the mountains, this cave. I could not believe what I had caused. It was beyond my worst nightmare. Living things were dying everywhere the humans went, and I could not leave the cave to stop them because their magic uncontrolled was too powerful.

A long time later, I know not when, Parlo ventured up to my cave. While I was imprisoned there, I had been spending my time watching the metal town. There seemed to be no peace there now. Everything was in chaos. Parlo came to me with tears in his eyes.

He knew what demons he had created, but he could not stop them now. He pleaded with me for an alternate spell, a less dangerous one. At this point, I did not want any humans to have magic but since he already knew the powerful Awakening spell, I figured giving him a lesser one would be all I could do, as long as he would never use the other again. The original spell I had given him Awakened full, raw, elemental power in every person. I now saw that only some could handle it, so the new spell I gave him worked on only those who could.

As I taught him this spell, an enormous explosion caught our attention. We hurried over to the rim of the cave and looked down towards the town. To our surprise, and Parlo's horror, the entire place had been engulfed in a fireball of epic proportions. It seemed to have come from the metal pillar as it was returning to the surface. Everything was destroyed. The entire town lay in ruin.

We returned to the lake, but it was no longer habitable. I checked beneath the water to see what damage had been done, and I saw that the portal was no longer there. The machine that had created it was cracked. I was content at least that no more humans would arrive, but Parlo was very distressed. He knew that his kind had destroyed my home, and his guilt ate at him. Without the fish from the lake, which had all been killed by the explosion, I would either starve or have to move away. Parlo could not bear making me leave, so he arranged for fish to be sent up from the town along the ocean coastline. Telling him how long I could live, he decided to make this arrangement permanent, so that fish would always be left at this cave.

Afterwards, his town destroyed, Parlo left for Jokatone, which had been settled recently. There he set up the battle school and trained the young in the use of magic. Before he died, he passed down his knowledge of the Awakening spell to another, and magic has remained in the hands of some humans up to this very day.

The other men who had been Awakened spread throughout the world, helping at times, but mostly hurting. Eventually, they all died out, leaving Jokatone as the only area in the world to still have magic.

This was the beginning of humans on this planet. I know not specifically where they came from before, but they are not native here. My gift turned into a curse, and I am forever paying for it. I do not know if there will ever come a day when my curse is lifted."

Chapter 19

The end of the tale was greeted by silence. Finally, Caleth spoke.

"That is a thought provoking story, Marinteya," he said, "but I think I know the problem."

"What?" Marinteya asked.

"You gave humans magic too soon," he stated. "They were not ready for it because they did not have time to become part of this world yet."

"Perhaps you are correct, but why should I Awaken another when magic in the hands of humans has destroyed this world?"

"Because maybe this time we can handle magic," Caleth answered. "We can use it to help rather than hurt."

"Jokatone still has magic," Marinteya stated. "Is that not enough?"

"Jokatone does not use its magic as it should," Caleth replied. "Its only use for magic is in war, which is not just the fault of humans but also of Hranthus and of the vashaka who governs Quantoff. Magic should not be used in such a way. This destructive use of magic has created the Desolate Fields and driven the native kralthaks into a hole underground. Give Granthwin magic, and she can use it to avoid fighting. Perhaps we can put a stop to the malevolent use of magic and help the kralthaks reclaim their lost lands."

"Maybe you are right," Marinteya said, "but maybe you are not. I will have to think about it, but whatever I may decide you will have to do something for me first. Fish have stopped arriving from the ocean-side town. The humans have broken their promise to me. Go and fix this problem, and I will tell you my decision upon your return."

"We will do this for you," Caleth stated.

The company gathered by the exit to the chamber. Suddenly, Caleth turned back to Marinteya.

"May you always be regarded highly," he said, which was the common kralthak farewell.

Marinteya looked taken aback for a moment and intrigued. After a moment's hesitation, she responded with the correct reply: "May all respect your worth."

Caleth then left the room, with the rest of the group following. It took them a while to find their way through the tunnel complex, but eventually they reached the outside world. Once they had left the cave behind them, Lunan turned to Caleth and spoke.

"How are we going to find the ocean-side town?" he asked. "We have no idea where it is."

"I got a chance to look at some of the maps in there," Caleth explained, "and I happened to notice a town near a large expanse of water. I'm assuming that is the town we seek, since it is not too far from here. We need to head southeast."

So that they did, travelling for many days over the mountains. From the peak of the last one in their way, they could just see the sparkle of water on the horizon, more water in one place than they had ever seen before. After they descended from the peak, they had only to travel for three more days before reaching the town.

As they approached their destination, they saw that it looked just like any town in Jokatone or Quantoff, except for a few metal buildings, mostly falling down at this point. They walked beneath an arch to enter, next to an untended gatehouse, and a sign informed them that they had entered Ficcula. The streets were filled with an assortment of people, and the smell of liquor hung on the air. The town was large; it had expanded much since the time of its founding because the people were content to remain in one place instead of spreading out to establish various other villages in the area.

The company asked a semi-respectable looking person where they could find the town's leader, and with only a couple of wrong turns, they managed to reach the man they sought. They located him inside a greatly decorated building that looked strikingly out of place amid the squalor that surrounded it. He was an arrogant-looking man who had a tendency to flare his nostrils from time to time, and his face seemed permanently etched in a self-righteous smirk.

"Who are you and what do you want?" he growled irritably as they approached.

"We will inform you of our business shortly," Caleth answered, "but first, are you the leader of Ficcula?"

"Yeah," the man replied, "but I don't recognize you. Where are you from?"

"The lands of Jokatone and Quantoff," Lunan supplied.

"Ugh," the man said, "my people don't ever go there. Not good to get in the middle of a war, if you know what I mean."

"You have discontinued a tradition from the ancient days," Granthwin stated. "We are here to see it is renewed."

"What are you talking about?" the man grunted.

"You were to have fish delivered to a cave in the mountains," Flioba stated.

"Oh, that," the man said with mock surprise. "Why in the world do we need to keep doing that?"

"This old tradition must be continued," Caleth stated. "It is the least you could do after our people drove the rightful inhabitants of this world into holes in the ground."

"I have no idea of what you are talking about," the man said, "and I have no intention of delivering fish to some cave. What a waste!"

"But you have to…" Flioba pleaded.

"Why?" the man asked disdainfully. "The old legends said that if we stopped delivering the fish, destruction would rain down upon us, but does it look like that happened? I took a chance when I stopped that tradition, and nothing bad has ever happened. The legends lied."

"If it is destruction you wish to see," Caleth stated, "then I will give you destruction."

He raised both hands up towards the ceiling and uttered, "*Konhekto fachalan kua piktol naual eptona hre shala.*" He dropped his right hand down to point at the ground next to Ficcula's leader, and a lightning bolt smashed through the ceiling and struck where he pointed, leaving a burning, gaping hole in the ceiling and a large scorch mark on the floor. The man jumped backwards, singed and blinded by the bolt's close proximity.

"A wizard!" he shrieked. He had forgotten that Jokatone trained spellcasters.

"Next time I won't miss," Caleth stated, attempting to look as intimidating as possible.

"Alright, alright," the man stammered, "I'll do what you want, just don't hurt me. You can kill everyone in this town for all I care, just don't hurt me, please." He looked like a miserable wretch.

"You disgust me," Caleth said. "Just make sure the fish is delivered, and if you ever are tempted to forget the old tradition again, remember this little incident as a warning."

"Yes, yes," the man whimpered, "I'll send the fish. You can even take some yourself from the docks. Just leave me in peace."

Caleth was about to refuse the offer of taking fish himself when Lunan stopped him.

"We may need to bring some back to show we were successful," he stated.

Caleth saw the sense in this and agreed.

"Don't forget," he said to the man before turning and walking out of the room with the others.

They walked to the docks without delay and, though it took some convincing to get the dock workers to let them, quickly filled their bags with some of the fish. They didn't take too many, not wanting to be over-encumbered on the journey back. With a little magic on Flioba's part, the fish were preserved so they wouldn't smell on the way.

The company was slowed down by rain; it took them much longer to get back to the cave than it did to get to the town. With a little magic, they managed to stay dry, but they had to wait out the storm. Eventually, however, they did manage to reach the cave, and it was not long after that they found Marinteya.

Chapter 20

When they entered the chamber, Marinteya was pouring over old maps in her kralthak form. The company paused for a moment, unsure of how to proceed. Eventually, Lunan broke the awkward silence by clearing his throat. Marinteya turned towards them.

"So?" she inquired.

"We did it," Caleth replied.

"Here are the fish," Granthwin put in. "Where do you want them?"

"Just put them in that corner," Marinteya said, gesturing. As they did that, she asked, "And how is the town? I haven't been over in that area for quite a while now."

"A sprawling dump with a corrupt leader," Lunan answered in a disgusted tone.

"Sounds the same as ever," Marinteya stated.

"What is your decision?" Caleth asked, anxious to hear what she would say.

131

"After much consideration," she began, "I have determined that humans have destroyed this world. But, my actions may have caused a tremendous part of this problem. Humans may be the destroyers of our native life, but my kind is not helping. In fact, vashakax are creating wars, as you well know. The entire planet is filled with corruption and violence. This may have been caused by humans, but I think maybe, just maybe, humans can correct their errors and help this planet. I have decided that I will take the chance to set things right and let humans show their worth. I sincerely hope that you will show me you deserve this."

"You will Awaken Granthwin?" Caleth inquired in amazed disbelief.

"No," Marinteya stated, "I will not. If I Awaken her, she will be too powerful. Power eats at a person; I cannot let that happen."

"But..." Caleth stuttered, "you said..."

"I will do you one better," Marinteya said. "I will teach you the Awakening spell."

"Me?" Caleth asked. "Why?"

"I see that you have good intentions and, I think, a bright intellect," she stated. "Also, as Kralthak-Saver I trust you will have good judgment in whom to Awaken. Please do not prove me wrong; the last chance for humanity rests in your hands."

Caleth was shocked into speechlessness. Did he really deserve this? Could he really be trusted to hold the second chance for humans and to make things right? Sure, he meant well, but so did Parlo, and look what he caused. There was only one thing Caleth was sure of: he would try his best. He only hoped it would be enough to right the wrongs of mankind.

Caleth was taken into another room to learn the spell. The room he entered was filled only with books, on shelves, in carefully stacked piles, and in heaps. Caleth made sure not to tread on any.

Marinteya taught him the spell rather quickly. It wasn't especially draining, but it was a lot to remember. Caleth thought he would be taught the same spell that had been cast on him when he first came to the battle school, but he could tell it was not exactly the same one. When he asked Marinteya about it, she told him that many years in solitude had given her time to develop a much more refined Awakening spell, although she had never thought she would use it, except on vashakax. This spell, she told him, could be used not only to Awaken elemental magic, but also to Awaken everyone else in the way best suited for them. It was a complicated spell meant to Awaken every person's deepest talents.

◊◊◊◊◊◊◊

Later, though he was unsure how much later since the lighting in the tunnels never changed, Caleth rose from his rest. Learning the spell had taken a long time, and once he had finished and rejoined his friends, they slept before any further action was taken. It was not good to do anything when exhausted, especially casting the Awakening spell, where one wrong word could mean death.

Caleth took Granthwin and Lunan into another chamber, leaving Flioba with Marinteya. Lunan was extremely surprised to be going, but interested at the same time. If they were to make things right, they would need all the help they could get, and if they all had magic, they had a huge advantage. Lunan seemed doubtful that it would work, but he figured that it wouldn't be a big deal to try. Caleth seated them on jewel embedded chairs he had found amid the piles of treasures. Marinteya didn't care if they touched her riches, as long as they didn't take off with any. Caleth took a deep breath, and then began the Awakening spell.

"Try to relax," he began. "This works better with a loosened mind. Ready?"

Granthwin and Lunan nodded.

"Alright," Caleth said, "here goes. Feel your inner self Awaken. *Awanin seyon.* Experience your mind becoming one for the first time. *Draktoneth kinowan ji seyon kua oniquon.* Listen to yourself as you never could before. *Ka horandir da seykino.* Do not fight with your inner spirit. *Nakan ka jikona di seyon.* Only time can bind it with your mind. *Draktoneth yewol kua dingra kinowan ji seyon.*"

This part was the same as in the Awakening spell cast on Caleth, except for a few words in the language of magic. Quazi helped Caleth channel his magic into Granthwin and Lunan, helping to break the mental barriers preventing the inner spirit from interacting with the mind. Soon they would be Awakened and be able to use magic to the same extent as Caleth and Flioba. Caleth continued with the spell. The next part was different from the Awakening spell cast upon him.

"Your mind will augment your talents," he spoke. "*Draktoneth seykino kua marheno chepax.* Feel the change in ability. *Ka lethos hepal de chepa.* Let your mind open to the world around you. *Ka kuilar seykino pritui da sristik.* Gain power but also knowledge. *Ka bathue niktuafal lir pluno jikan.* Realize your full potential. *Ka kigrol zren pajik.*"

Caleth raised his arms over his head and curled his right hand into a circular shape as he brought his hands together, his left hand surrounding the circle of his right. As soon as he did this, a beam of golden light was emitted from the circle made by Caleth's hands. This beam was directed at Quazi, who swelled to an enormous size and split the beam into two, one shining on Granthwin's face and the other on Lunan's. Over each spot where the beams struck, a giant pileated woodpecker appeared, consisting completely of golden light. The birds raised their wings into a regal pose over the humans below before taking flight upwards and disappearing.

According to Marinteya, woodpeckers were a symbol of intelligence and the life cycle to the original kralthaks. Most of the kralthaks nowadays had probably never seen one.

This marked the end of the spell. Caleth let his arms down in exhaustion. For such a long spell, however, it wasn't as tiring as it could have been. He bade Granthwin and Lunan to rise from the chairs.

"So," he said with a smile on his face, "how does it feel?"

"I feel a little more alert," Granthwin replied, "but not a whole lot more."

"Same here," Lunan stated. "So, what now?"

"I don't know," Caleth said. "Try to cast a spell, I guess."

"Alright," Granthwin agreed, "how?"

"I'm not exactly sure," Caleth responded. "This wasn't the same Awakening spell cast on me. I don't know for sure what you both will be able to do. I guess you could start by trying a lesser fireball. I'll show you how first, and then you both try."

Caleth pointed at a bare patch of ground and spoke, "*Vi konhekto zargath de kethronet.*" He then quickly formed his hand into a ball and exploded his fingers outwards in a smooth motion. Where he directed, a small orb of fire appeared and blasted outwards slightly, leaving a small scorch mark but nothing major.

"Okay," Caleth said, "now you try it."

Though they tried over and over again, neither Granthwin nor Lunan managed to replicate Caleth's feat. He went over the gestures with them, the words, and even the thoughts associated with the spell, but they could not seem to cast it. Eventually, they gave up.

"I guess fire isn't your thing," Caleth said, somewhat doubtful that the Awakening spell had even worked.

Lunan decided to take a break, but Granthwin was determined

and wanted to continue attempting other things.

"You said I was good at earth magic before," Granthwin stated. "Maybe I could try that?"

"Hmm, good idea," Caleth said. "You did seem to have an affinity for it. Try this."

He reached out his arm towards the ground again, but this time he held his hand palm up with fingers pointing towards the ceiling. He wiggled his fingers and raised his arm as he spoke, "*Vi konhekto evi suith.*" Where he had indicated, a very small maple tree sprouted from the ground. It grew to a foot tall and put out tiny leaves, looking like a miniature adult tree.

Now it was Granthwin's turn. She concentrated extremely hard at a spot next to Caleth's maple and did just as he had moments before. This time, it actually worked. To Granthwin's amazement, a tree grew out of the ground and rose to about the same height as Caleth's. This tree was not a maple; it was an apple tree, complete with tiny apples. Curious about how they would taste, she tried one of them and found it to be indeed delicious.

Caleth smiled at Granthwin, and she smiled back. Overcome with emotion, they embraced and laughed light-heartedly. The Awakening spell had worked. Granthwin could use magic. Their adventure thus far had been a success.

However, the magic Awakened in Lunan was still a mystery. They knew not what form it would take, but Granthwin's success gave them renewed vigor. He kept trying different spells that Caleth demonstrated, but to no avail. He did not seem magically inclined, and they were running out of possibilities. Finally, Caleth thought of an idea they had not yet attempted.

"How about you try casting through your sword," he suggested.

Lunan was willing to try. He held his sword above his head and spoke the words that Caleth supplied. He uttered, "*Konhekto zargath kua grothar nitko.*" As he finished speaking, flames spurted up from the hilt of Lunan's sword and swirled around the blade before conjoining at the tip. He had enchanted his sword with fire.

Surprised, Lunan dropped his blade. As soon as it left his hand, the flames went out, and an ordinary sword clanged against the ground. Lunan picked up his weapon with wonder. He had actually done it. He had not thought that it was possible and believed the Awakening spell hadn't worked and was just an illusion, but he had actually created flames around his sword. It was real.

All of this excitement and spellcasting tired out Caleth, Granthwin, and Lunan, and they slept although the day was not quite over. Flioba bided her time looking over old books and talking with Marinteya. Soon they would have to leave this cave and embark out on their own. It was up to them to make things right.

◊◊◊◊◊◊◊

Caleth woke early the following morning. When he found Marinteya, she was studying one of her maps again. Caleth approached and saw that it consisted of Jokatone and Quantoff and their immediate surroundings. Marinteya turned at his entrance into the chamber.

"I have been thinking," she began.

"Yes?" Caleth asked.

"If you are going to fix humans' ways and eliminate corruption, you will need a base," she stated.

"That makes sense," Caleth agreed. "But where?"

"I have been surveying the maps," she said, "and I think I may have found a suitable area. It is west of Jokatone, close to being in between Jokatone and Quantoff. Separating the area from inhabited lands is a great river; I believe you have heard of the Rippling River."

"I have."

"Well," Marinteya continued, pointing at a location on the map, "at this point the Rippling River is joined by the Shimmering River, which bends here, creating an area that it nearly completely surrounds. This renders the area very defensible. If my maps are still accurate, there is a clearing directly at this spot. It would be the perfect place for a home base."

"That sounds like a good idea," Caleth said, "but who would live there? A town cannot consist solely of four people. We would need others to join us."

"This is for you to decide," Marinteya stated. "Perhaps you will have thought of something by the time you get there."

"Maybe," Caleth responded doubtfully.

"Here," Marinteya spoke, "I have drawn a rough sketch of this map to take with you. Perhaps I will visit you there in person some day." She handed him a rolled-up scroll. "I hope for everyone's sake that you can accomplish what is set before you".

Once the rest of the company had awoken, they gathered their belongings and made ready to depart. Caleth informed them of their destination, which they were all too ready to reach so they could rest for awhile. Adventuring left one weary. After bidding their farewells to Marinteya, they set off once again, hoping for fair weather and an easy journey.

Chapter 21

For many days, they traversed the mountains, following Marinteya's map. It rained often, dampening the company's spirits as they trudged about in soggy clothing. The going was difficult with steep slopes, crowded undergrowth, and treacherous ledges, but eventually they made it through.

With the mountains behind them, they thought that the going would get easier, but in front of them lay the Endless Forest. From atop the last peak in their path, they could see the vast canopy spreading beneath them with little holes where light could filter through. It would be dim in the forest, and dangerous; Caleth had heard that there were strange creatures that lurked in the depths. They would have to be careful.

They descended into the forest below, moving slowly to avoid tripping. Before long, they were beneath the tree tops and in a completely different landscape. The air was humid, and the forest was gloomy. Shafts of light hit the ground every now and then, but for the most part it was dark. The forest floor was covered with rotting leaves and mushrooms sprouting from fallen trees. Bird calls rang out from the branches above. The entire place was almost completely alive. There were more types of insects, frogs, and birds than the company had ever seen before. There were few mammals visible, but the ones they saw were bizarre. Most never came down to the forest floor, but there were some that hunted between the tree trunks.

The group had difficulty continuing in their course due to large trees and other undergrowth in their way, but they managed to push forward through the dimly lit, tree lined labyrinth. Occasionally they would find a bush with berries or a tree with other fruits, and these they would eat slowly in an attempt to savor the taste. Previously they had been obtaining food magically, but it never tasted as good as when fresh.

Along the way, Granthwin and Lunan practiced spellcasting under the guidance of Caleth and Flioba. In time, they came to be quite good at their particular magics, but it was difficult to become entirely proficient without all the proper words and specific tutelage. Lunan had an easier time than Granthwin. Many of the spells Caleth knew offhand Lunan could easily cast on his sword, enchanting it with any number of elements and effects. However, earth magic was much more complicated. It required many words to get across a simple spell, and even with the combined knowledge of Caleth and Flioba, they still didn't know enough. Sure, she could summon certain plants, but when it came to offensive magic, they didn't know exactly what to do. Perhaps eventually, they could come up with useful spells that she could cast, but for now they were forced to stick to basics and mostly unhelpful spells.

Although the forest seemed the same in every direction and they often thought they were going in circles, the company was able to navigate using the map and a Compass spell cast by Caleth. It was one of the spells included in the back of the book he had received from his former teacher. He sometimes wondered how the people he knew back at the battle school were getting along and what his parents had thought when they found out he had left, but he could not think these thoughts for long. It was never good to wonder how things could have been, so he forced himself to think only of the present.

Luckily, he had Granthwin to help him keep his mind off things. He delighted in her presence and was pretty sure she liked him too. Yet, he was unsure of how he should act around her, and they mainly talked. Whenever they would brush up against each other momentarily, it would make Caleth's day. Granthwin seemed a little shy herself. She would kind of hang near him when they walked, and he would try to do the same, but there were often long periods of silence. Even with this, though, Caleth felt great, but he often longed to hold her hand or even exchange a kiss.

Lunan and Flioba had no trouble expressing their affection. They hung over each other and held hands while they walked. Caleth often saw them hugging and leaning against one another, and he wondered why it was so easy for them. Caleth's interactions with Granthwin mostly consisted of exchanging smiles, though he used the excuse of helping with her spellcasting to get closer to her and sit up against her.

Even with these interparty relationships, all members of the company were still able to talk to each other most of the time, without worrying about interrupting others. They discussed their plans for the town and their goals for the future, along with more immediate situations. Caleth always found it easy to talk out loud in general and to Lunan especially, but it was much more difficult for him to talk with Granthwin. Possibly, he thought, it was because they had never really declared their feelings for each other and were unsure of how the other actually felt. Regardless, most of their personal conversations were only over trivial things and they quickly ran out of topics for discussion. Caleth hoped they would eventually become more accustomed to one another.

It wasn't too long before they reached the Rippling River. It cut through the Endless Forest in a wide band, and they would have to cross it to continue their journey. It would have been easier if they could have followed the river to get to their destination, but unfortunately it also ran through Quantoff, separating the kingdom into two sections: one large and one small. At this point, they did not want to worry about meeting any people in Quantoff, so they decided to skirt its border until they reached the Shimmering River.

Crossing the river was not an easy task. Lunan proposed building a raft out of fallen trees, but the wood they found was damp and would not work well. Nearly everything was moist in the forest. Eventually, Caleth thought of a spell that would be good practice for Granthwin. He instructed her in what to do, hoping it would actually work. It was not always easy to come up with spells, but he managed fairly well most of the time.

Granthwin looked out across the river and took a deep breath. She was not entirely confident in her spellcasting abilities yet, but she wanted to make Caleth proud. He had instructed her to create a land bridge, and a land bridge she would create; she only hoped it would actually span the river. As Caleth had instructed her, Granthwin arched both arms out in front of her as if she were trying to show someone how to dive with her hands. While she did this, she spoke, "*Konhekto naual kua heklandel elthnik plep arlan.*" To her delight, a bridge of earth rose in front of her and continued to grow as it extended across the river. To her dismay, it continued to rise vertically as well as horizontally and did not descend to the other bank of the river. It would not work to get them across; she had failed and could not even bring herself to look into Caleth's eyes.

"Cancel it," Caleth instructed her, and she sadly complied. "I think I have an idea," he continued. "The reason most of my spells work is because of Quazi here." He gestured to the quazicar as it hovered next to his head. "I don't see any reason why he can't help the rest of you too."

Caleth told Quazi what he wanted him to do, and, although he had no idea whether the quazicar understood, he told Granthwin to try the spell again. She dismally repeated what she had done a moment ago, but this time Quazi must have altered the spell based on the picture in Granthwin's mind. He expanded, and the bridge worked successfully.

"Well, that could be a lot of help," Caleth stated, and the rest agreed.

◊◊◊◊◊◊◊

After travelling west for some time, the company eventually turned north once they were sure they had gotten past the western edge of the Quantoffan border. From there, they would move due north to reach their destination.

With little trouble thus far, the group let their guard down as they trekked along, walking more boldly and having a good time. They figured that if anything was going to attack them, it would have done so by then. However, they spoke too soon.

They were travelling through a slightly better lit section of the forest when it happened. Around them were smaller trees, slowly growing up to fill the hole in the forest canopy. Some of these trees had delicious fruits hanging from their limbs. They were brilliantly colored with bright yellows and blues and reds. They decided to rest there for awhile since the air was less humid and the warm sun on their faces felt wonderful after days spent in the dark depths of the woods. They picked many of the fruits, eating some immediately, and saving others for later. It was only afterwards that they realized these trees were carefully planted and tended, and not wild like they had originally thought.

They were delighting in their current situation when they heard the first sounds of danger approaching. From high up in the canopy came a loud screeching and growling, coming nearer and nearer. At first they thought nothing of it; there were many sounds in the forest, and they nearly never saw the sources of them. This time the sound continued to approach and was joined by others, increasing the shrieking and howling. Beginning to get worried, the company drew into a protective circle and readied their weapons and their minds. Before long, the sounds surrounded them.

It was not long thereafter when they first saw the creatures. A primate leapt from the trees and soared directly over their heads, clutching a stick and yammering loudly. The company thought the monkey would pass them by, uninterested, as most creatures did in the forest, but this creature seemed angry. As it went over them, it launched its stick like a spear, piercing the ground at Caleth's feet. Apparently, this monkey meant business.

As the first monkey landed and scurried back into the trees, many more primates leapt from the branches, directly at the humans. Caleth was worried. The monkeys were quick and difficult to target. This was their home, and they were ready to defend it with their lives. The carnage would be devastating.

They could not risk fire in the forest, so they quickly turned to other means in order to defend themselves. Caleth shot missiles of ice at the monkeys as they came, shouting, "*Konhekto erkto di hethwaf.*" Icicles flew through the air towards the raging apes, impaling those they struck. Flioba used wind to slap the monkeys out of the air. *"Konhekto panthuerno kua piktol hikit,"* she uttered. Lunan shouted, *"Konhekto fachalan kua grothar nitko,"* enchanting his sword with lightning. Granthwin could not think of an offensive spell quickly, and so she solely used her rapier, striking again and again at the incoming primates.

For a while, the company seemed to be managing, but the monkeys were fierce and quick. They could dodge attacks that would have killed a human. Still, the party's magic seemed to be holding them at bay.

This all changed when one of the monkeys thrust a stick deep into Flioba's leg. She screamed, letting down her guard, and then they were all over her, stabbing and biting and clawing. Lunan yelled in dismay and charged the apes, his sword flashing. Many monkeys went down, convulsing due to the electricity that raced up and down his sword, but the damage was done. Flioba lay on the ground, shaking slightly and crying, her blood running into the dirt. Caleth and Granthwin surrounded Flioba and Lunan, giving Lunan time to work over Flioba's wounds. Unfortunately, he had little snaplora fluid left, and was running out of options.

"What is the magic word for 'heal'?" he shouted, desperate for any help he could get.

"Fornijka," Caleth answered, "but I doubt it will work; it takes a long time to learn how to heal properly with magic."

Lunan didn't care, there was little left for him to try, and Flioba was running out of time. *"Fornijka,"* he spoke softly, holding her hand tenderly. Nothing happened. Lunan cursed, was there nothing he could do? A moment later, something began to happen. A green glow spread from where Lunan clutched her hand and extended all over her body. It pooled where her cuts and other injuries were, slowly binding them back together. Flioba was healed.

Unfortunately, while Flioba was mending, another member of

the group was injured. Having two less people to fend off monkey attacks proved to be disastrous. The monkeys attacked too quickly and too often; they overwhelmed Granthwin. One minute, she was stabbing and slicing with her rapier, the next, she was lying on the ground, coughing blood. An errant stick had slipped past her defenses and speared her in the chest. She let loose a blood-curdling screech and spit blood onto the ground.

"No!" Caleth screamed, but there was nothing he could do. He had to defend everyone in the group by himself. Seeing Granthwin's life drain away from her as she lay on the ground put a fury in Caleth. In his rage, he uttered a spell so massive that he had never contemplated it before.

"*Konhekto hethwaf de slana do suelnak kua buelnos ji kua piktol hikitix, hevkel kli masos!*" he shouted at the top of his voice, bringing his hands from the front of his body to the back in the path of a circle. As he did so, an enormous dome of ice appeared over his head, encasing his friends. After forming, it expanded at a rapid rate, striking the monkeys on all sides, leaving them dead, before shattering into millions of ice shards. The ice did no damage to the trees, leaving them unharmed, and the shards fell to the sides of the company so they were not injured further. Only a few monkeys survived that blast, and those that did quickly scampered away into the forest in fear.

The spell should have entirely drained Caleth and left him weak and helpless, but his fear and concern for Granthwin gave him strength. He knelt by her side and felt her pulse. It was faint and slowing.

"No! No!" he exclaimed. "This can't be happening!"

But it was. Her eyelids flickered for a moment, giving Caleth hope, but then they closed. Her chest heaved for the last time. Her pulse stopped. Granthwin was dead!

Chapter 22

"NO!!!" Caleth screamed at the sky, a cry of anguish and despair.

Lunan rushed over. He tried to cast healing spells and restart her heart, but it was too late. Granthwin was gone. They couldn't believe it. Flioba stood up and walked over, seeming to be completely recovered. How was that fair? They stood mournfully beside Caleth as he cried tears of utter sorrow down upon Granthwin. There was nothing left that they could do.

Caleth wept for hours until he passed out across her body due to exhaustion. Lunan and Flioba were upset, but nowhere near the grief-stricken state that Caleth was in. They took care of the camp and made dinner while he cried. They offered him some, but he refused. Still they wouldn't take no for an answer, knowing how important it was that he received proper nutrition, so he eventually choked down a small chunk of food and some water. It was quite a while before he woke up.

When he came to, he was draped over Granthwin's cold body. Remembering what had happened, he cried anew before forcing himself to suck up the pain and deal with the present. It was then that he realized that roots were slowly wrapping themselves around Granthwin's body, some effect of her earth magic affinity, he supposed. Before she was completely encased, he sorrowfully removed the eternal fire gem amulet from around his neck and slipped it over Granthwin's. If it really symbolized love, it was fitting for her to have it. In solitude, he watched as the roots completely covered her corpse and dragged her down into the earth, creating a sort of living coffin.

Caleth sadly gazed at the spot where her body had lain. Thoughts raced through his head. He thought of what could have been: marrying Granthwin, having a family; he thought of the things he had never done: kissed her, told her he loved her, held her hand; and he wondered what he would do without her. He never realized how much he loved her until she was gone.

Sorrowfully, he made himself get to his feet and join Lunan and Flioba. Would things ever be the same? Lunan wanted to push on, to get as much distance between them and this spot as they could, but Caleth would not leave yet; he was not ready. So Lunan and Flioba waited and bided their time as Caleth pulled himself together.

It was several days later before he was ready to depart. They gathered their things and took down their camp. Soon they were ready to be on their way. Caleth did not look back as they set off, but Flioba did.

"Caleth, look," she said, pointing back to where Granthwin had died.

Caleth dismally turned his head to look. Oddly, the living coffin where Granthwin's body was held had returned to the surface.

"Just give me one moment," Caleth stated, before rushing over to it.

As he approached, he saw that the top of the coffin was open. Caleth looked over the top and saw Granthwin's body lain out like a viewing. He sorrowfully reached out his hand and tenderly touched her cheek. To his surprise, it was warm. Startled, he felt for her pulse, and was shocked to find that there was one. As he watched, color returned to her body. It seemed to be spreading from the eternal fire gem, which was slowly fading in color to a deep black.

"Granthwin?" he whispered softly.

She opened her eyes and smiled up at him. The earth had healed her with the magic in the eternal fire gem!

"Caleth," she said faintly.

"Oh Granthwin!" Caleth exclaimed. "I love you so much, you have no idea!"

"I love you too, Caleth," she whispered, smiling. "Help me up."

Caleth helped her to her feet. She was a bit shaky but overall in good health. The stab wound was gone, leaving only a scar where the gash had once been. Beaming at each other's declaration of their love, they kissed. It was the most beautiful thing Caleth had ever experienced, and he never wanted it to end. However, they reluctantly pulled apart.

"You...you were dead," Caleth stammered.

"It was not yet my time," Granthwin replied, and she never gave a clearer explanation than that.

Seeing Granthwin alive and well, Lunan and Flioba hurried over, both embracing Granthwin in their joy.

"You're alive!" Flioba exclaimed.

The joyfulness filled them from that moment and stayed with them for a long time afterwards. They knew how lucky they were to have Granthwin with them, but they never understood how it had happened. Caleth was ecstatic in his joy and kissed Granthwin again before they unpacked. Although Granthwin was alive, she was weak and needed rest. It would be many more days before they could move on.

◊◊◊◊◊◊◊◊

They arrived at the Shimmering River a week after Granthwin recovered. Caleth could see how the river got its name: the sunlight cascaded off its surface, creating a sparkling effect that made the whole river seem to glisten. It was easily traversed by a land bridge created by Granthwin. After crossing, she let the bridge fall away behind her so no creatures could follow them.

Now that they had crossed the river, they were at the point where Marinteya had told them to build a town. Caleth now understood her reasoning. The region seemed to be one of the only places in the forest devoid of trees for any significant area. There were only two trees in the clearing; they were large and old and leaned against each other, creating a space between like a triangular doorway. The glade was also largely surrounded by a bend in the river, creating a defensible location with access to fish for food. It was the perfect location to erect their home base.

They quickly constructed their first building, which they used as shelter while they built others. Later, they built two houses, one for Caleth and Granthwin, and one for Lunan and Flioba. They used the first building they had constructed as a public hall where they could gather. Granthwin cast a Perpetual Re-growth spell on the trees that bordered the clearing so that as they cut them down to build their homes and other buildings, new ones would quickly sprout and fill the spaces left by the old ones. This was a complicated spell that Caleth didn't know. When he asked her about it, she said she had been given knowledge from the earth while it healed her.

Quazi seemed to really enjoy the area, swooping around with joy. Caleth realized that it must have been a spot similar to his original home. As Quazi flew around the clearing, Caleth was surprised to see another quazicar join him from out of the trees. They danced together in the clearing and were soon joined by others. It seemed to be an entire colony of quazicars. Caleth was happy to see Quazi with his own kind, but was saddened to think he might leave; they had been through so much together. But Quazi didn't leave, and neither did the other quazicars. They stayed on in the clearing with the humans, sometimes hovering playfully, and other times helping the spellcasters when the mood took them.

At first the humans were satisfied by their small village, but they soon yearned to hear the voices of others and build a real town, one populated by a large number of people. It was lonely with only four people in the middle of the forest. However, it would be difficult to get people to come from Jokatone and Quantoff. The people there were largely war-like and wouldn't be the right types for their mission to make things right.

Caleth looked at the woods around him and at the sparkling river with its cool water. He thought of how odd it was that this was what the Desolate Plains had once looked like, with the kralthaks hunting in the brush and basking in the sun; now they were reduced to feeding off the dead and living where the light never reached.

"Of course!" Caleth said aloud. "The kralthaks!"

"What?" Granthwin asked, confused. They were sitting together outside of their house.

"That's who should live in our town with us," Caleth responded. "Who better to set things right than those who lived here originally?"

"That'll never work," Flioba remarked, overhearing the conversation as she carried water back from the river. "The kralthaks don't have anybody to spare to send out here. You heard what the Great Lord Thowgotel said: they don't even have enough kralthaks to grow their own food."

"I have a solution," Caleth stated. "I can conjure a portal between here and the kralthak den. Then they can move between the two places without worrying about having to spare anyone. If the den is attacked, all the kralthaks could rush in and defend it. They could grow food out here, and hunt. It would be good for them to be back in the open air."

"That sounds like an excellent plan," Granthwin spoke. "Do you know how to cast such a spell?"

"I do," Caleth replied. "I watched my teacher conjure a portal once."

"Then we should do it," Flioba agreed, "but we should first ask Lunan for his views on the matter."

They waited until Lunan returned from finding firewood and then told him of their plan. He thought it was a good idea, so they began the preparations at once. Before casting the spell, they thought it would be a good idea if they had some kind of offering, so they went hunting in the woods and returned with several plump animals that had been feasting on a berry bush. Caleth then readied the spell.

He had chosen the triangular area between the two trees in the clearing as the site for the portal. The trees would help hold up the portal and keep it there. Having chosen a location, he then began the spell. He traced the perimeter of the triangular area with his finger as he uttered, "*Wazak huelnef da niblo do kralthoukix ji agrakar di fachalan.*" A dark mass gathered on the perimeter of the region and slowly filled it in, creating an opaque shape. Then lightning leapt from Caleth's outstretched arms and dove deep into the void, briefly covering the entire area before receding into the center and disappearing. Moments passed as the portal rippled. Then suddenly it cleared, revealing not the other side of the glade, but instead the inside of the kralthak den. It had worked.

Kralthaks were gathering on the other side of the portal, and they brandished their weapons at the perceived threat of Caleth and the others looking in. They growled savagely and seemed like they would attack, but Caleth took charge of the situation.

"Calm," he said. "I am Saroofachtenel." He used the kralthak word that he had been taught for Kralthak-Saver.

The kralthaks visibly relaxed, but they were still on edge.

"Caleth?" a kralthak asked from the back of the group.

At first Caleth couldn't tell who had said it, but then he recognized the person in the crowd.

"The Great Lord Thowgotel!" he exclaimed. "It's good to see you. How have things been?"

The kralthaks calmed at this, seeing that he really was a friend of the kralthaks. They backed away from the portal, leaving Caleth and his companions alone facing Thowgotel, who looked thinner than when they had last seen him.

"Things are not well, Caleth," Thowgotel responded. "Since you last saw us, food has gotten scarcer and many of us are starving. To make matters worse, an undead creature recently attacked our den, killing several of our finest warriors. I do not know how many more years we can survive in these conditions."

"That is not good," Caleth stated. "However, I may be able to help. I have a proposition for King Filfwander, if I can see him."

"Any help you can give would be greatly appreciated," Thowgotel replied. "But how will you get to him?"

Caleth stepped through the portal, its fluid parting where he pushed through and remaining whole behind him.

"I'll follow you," Caleth stated, to Thowgotel's amazement.

Caleth stepped into the hallway clutching the animals they had caught. Apparently, the portal had formed in an empty storeroom. Caleth's friends stayed behind and let him handle the situation. Thowgotel led Caleth into a private room, where King Filfwander was sitting on a luxurious chair, scowling as he choked down tiny plants and unappetizing insects.

Caleth bowed low before approaching the King. Once Filfwander told him to stand, he brought forth the animals they had caught and gave them as gifts to the King. King Filfwander was delighted, but to Caleth's surprise he did not eat the animals himself; he sent them to be divided up among the kralthaks.

"So what is this proposition I hear you have?" King Filfwander inquired.

"I know you are in dire straits," Caleth stated, "and I have come to help."

"How so?"

"I have opened a portal between here and a glade in the Endless Forest where my friends and I are erecting a town. I have learned of your history. I know you originally lived in the forest, where you could hunt and live in the open air. You were the leaders of the world before humans came. I am now offering you a chance to reclaim your former glory. My friends and I are determined to set things right. Humans have done many wrongs to this planet. We hope to correct these. I am offering you a chance to join in our mission. If you would like, you can join us in our town and live among us aboveground where the sun shines. What do you say?"

"It's tempting, it really is, but this den belonged to the kralthaks of ancient times. I could not abandon it to go prancing through the woods."

"But that's the beauty of it, you don't have to," Caleth explained. "The portal will stay open, allowing a permanent gateway between there and here. If there is an emergency, the kralthaks in the forest could quickly return to the den."

"I don't know. I cannot in good consciousness abandon this den. It is where I was born and where I have ruled for many years."

Caleth attempted to argue that the King would not really be abandoning the den, but King Filfwander stopped him.

"However," the King continued, "I would be willing to send a group to live among you. We need food, and it would be good for the kralthaks to bond with your people. I will send the Great Lord Thowgotel to lead them, since he is already known to you."

"Thank you," Caleth replied. "You are most generous."

"May you always be regarded highly," the King finished, signaling that it was time for Caleth to depart.

"May all respect your worth," Caleth responded properly and turned to leave.

Thowgotel led Caleth back to the portal, choosing his most trusted and loyal kralthaks to accompany him.

"Now," Caleth thought, "we have a chance to make things right."

Afterword

It took the kralthaks quite a while to adapt to life in the forest, but once they did, they became skilled hunters and experts at finding their way around the woods. The kralthaks who came to live in the forest rarely returned to the kralthak den, choosing instead to build houses and live with the humans. However, they never forgot to bring food back to their old home, and with it, the kralthaks were much better off than before and rarely scavenged the battlefield.

Caleth, Granthwin, Lunan, and Flioba were very happy to have the kralthaks' company, and with their help, they managed to build a truly thriving town. Many houses surrounded the original central hall that the humans had built, and the kralthaks took a variety of jobs, not all became hunters in the forest. Some became blacksmiths, farmers, cooks, animal raisers, butchers, guards, bakers, and many other occupations.

Caleth Awakened all of the kralthaks who lived aboveground,

and with their newfound magic, they excelled at all their crafts and professions. Magic became an integral part of the community, and casting spells became commonplace. Everyone had some talent that magic could enhance, and people typically took jobs that used their particular talent. In this way, nearly everything was done at a masterful level, and nearly everyone was satisfied with their particular magic abilities.

In time, the humans decided to scout out other humans who would be a beneficial part of the town, and who could help them in their mission. These humans were brought back to the town and trained to live among the kralthaks. Caleth Awakened each as they came, making each the best they could be.

Since magic became such a vital part of the town, the quazicars who had danced around the clearing when the humans first arrived stayed in the area. For some reason, they were drawn to magic and liked to bask in its aura. Some even bonded with humans as Quazi had with Caleth, and these helped to channel magic and shape it as was desired. Since Quazi had been around magic the longest, he had the greatest capacity for it. Although he would always stick with Caleth and help him out whenever he needed it, he also sometimes helped others with their magic as well.

Once magic became ingrained in the community, it bonded the people together and helped them live their lives. It allowed everyone to exist at their full potential. With magic, they could accomplish things that regular people could only dream of. As part of setting things back to the old ways, Caleth attempted to learn the full language of magic and insisted that everyone must learn it as fluently as possible. To the people of this town, magic and its language became a part of everyday life.

Though at first the humans and kralthaks had struggled to some extent at getting along, they soon learned they could coexist, and happily too. The town became a melting pot of those with good character. With the help of every man and kralthak in the town, they were capable of fighting the massive corruption and malevolent intent that gripped the lands. Together, they could fix a broken world.

A Guide to the Language of Magic

Tenses:

Infinitive-*kua* before verb

Present-no extra word

Past-*kui* before verb

Future-*kuo* before verb

Conditional-*ko* before verb

Imperative-*ka* before verb

Progressive-*kri* after verb

Passive Voice-*kra* after verb

Perfect-*kro* after verb

Subjects and Objects:

I/me-no word in front of verb, but *powna*

You (singular)-*laja*

He/him-*maso*

She/her-*masa*

It-*masu*

We/us-*lami*

You (plural)-*lajas*

They/them-*masos*

Possessives:

My-*pou*

Your (singular)-*laj*

His-*mos*

Her-*mas*

Its-*mus*

Our-*lam*

Your (Plural)-*lajix*

Their-*mosix*

Gerund: *kli* after word

Plural (-s): -*x* if after vowel, -*ix* if after consonant

Adjective to noun: add *ud*

Question Words:

Question word (goes in front of every question)-*vua*

Who?-*kol?*

What?-*kefra?*

Where?-*kental?*

When?-*klepa?*

Why?-*kuar?*

Which?-*kodri?*

How?-*kilthua?*

Word Translations

after-*puene*
against-*epinto*
air-*panthuanto*
also-*pluno*
animal-*vletnar*
ant-*miniquo*
area, region-*klion*
arm-*jokow*
aunt or uncle-*kejta*
aunt-*kejma*
autumn-*hethdrup*
away-*eftul*
baby-*jilano*
balance-*niwatan*
battle-*jikna*
bear-*guma*
because-*deri*
bee-*ziv*
between-*ikri*
big, long, large-*gri*
bird-*vasada*
birth-*jila*
boyfriend-*vueltek*
bridge-*elthnik*
brother-*amak*
bug-*riump*
building-*konj*
butterfly-*pardi*
cat-*mej*
center-*ogro*
change-*hepal*
chaos (disorder)-*trelthen*
child-*genol*
chipmunk-*kujak*

city, village, town, community-*quap*
cloud-*palo*
comeback-*jiklana*
complete, full-*zren*
completely-*zreno*
conjunction (and)-*ji*
conjunction (but)-*lir*
conjunction (or)-*jo*
cycle-*siklen*
daughter-*genal*
death-*jina*
deep-*dri*
deer-*ereda*
difficult, hard-*warni*
dog-*wolgi*
dolphin-*chamu*
dome-*suelnak*
dune-*kuiso*
Earth (Glathorin)-*Naua*
enemy-*hikuan*
energy-*krethnak*
eternally (for all time)-*zrena*
except-*kitho*
farm-*konjafithwith*
father-*huten*
finally-*iltini*
fire-*zargath*
first-*āzad*
fish-*skakui*
fly-*invati*
forest-*suik*
frog-*bunak*
fungus-*ploblub*
gas-*suta*

girlfriend-*vuelsek*

glade-*suithek*

goddess-*silfua*

god-*silfuo*

grandchild- *āzgenol*

granddaughter- *āzgenal*

grandfather- *āzhuten*

grandmother- *āzhusen*

grandparent- *āzhunen*

grandson- *āzgenop*

grass-*nelthou*

great aunt- *āzkejma*

great grandparent- *ĕzhunen*

great uncle- *āzkejla*

happiness-*wilkijud*

happy-*wilkij*

he/him-*maso*

help-*beknath*

here-*hofta*

her-*mas*

hill-*kuilo*

his-*mos*

home-*niblo*

house-*konjaniblo*

how-*kilthua*

human-*shaka*

husband-*voltek*

I/me-*powna*

ice, winter-*hethwaf*

if-*nima*

in order-*tiro*

inanimate-*fiokel*

inner spirit-*seyon*

insect-*īzump*

insulation-*quentiv*

intelligence-*jikan*

it-*masu*

its-*mus*

journey-*fuejo*

just, only-*olit*

kralthak-*kralthouk*

lake, pond-*arlag*

land, ground-*naual*

leader-*regathal*

leg-*ump*

less-*vi*

life-*jika*

light-*iltumin*

lightning-*fachalan*

like, as-*uja*

liquid-*futa*

man, male-*shala*

matter (the kind measured in grams)-
    okjadon

mind and inner spirit combined-
    seykino

mind-*kinowan*

missle-*erkto*

monkey-*hikit*

moon-*iltem*

mother-*husen*

moth-*pardu*

mountain-*karlo*

mouse-*ardo*

much, many, most, more, a lot-*ri*

my-*pou*

near-*eptona*

nephew-*kejtagenop*

newborn-*jilata*

niece-*kejtagenal*

nikian- *nikeana*

no (do not)-*nakan*

now-*alpunt*

number-*itho*

object, thing-*grefa*

occasionally-*lituan*

ocean-*arlos*

octopus-*jakiop*

old-*freklen*

order-*quono*

other-*yito*

our-*lam*

over-*plep*

pack, group-*horgak*

parent-*hunen*

path, road-*fieja*

pen-*flethra*

Plane of Elementals-*Kalamo*

plant-*braktua*

portal-*huelnef*

potential-*pajik*

power-*niktuafal*

precipitation-*ieagra*

preposition (by, answer to how?)-*dua*

preposition (for, duration)-*du*

preposition (from)-*due*

preposition (in)-*de*

preposition (of, possession, description of noun)-*do*

preposition (on)-*duo*

preposition (through)-*duene*

preposition (to, at, destination)-*da*

preposition (with, using)-*di*

problem-*yeko*

question word (goes in front of every question)-*vua*

rabbit-*jahi*

rainforest-*groufel*

rain-*ieagrou*

rat-*ardu*

ready (about to)-*veklow*

river-*arlan*

rock-*nebuan*

sadness-*tirsud*

sad-*tirs*

same-*giot*

set, fixed, certain-*permantua*

shape-*slana*

shark-*akshir*

she/her-*masa*

sibling-*amat*

since (duration)-*priol*

sister-*amas*

size-*miri*

sky-*panthul*

small-*evi*

snake-*nuvo*

snow-*ieagras*

solid-*kuta*

son-*genop*

sphere, ball, orb-*kethronet*

spider-*ōzump*

spouse-*volkek*

spring-*hethglip*

squid-*menoud*

squirrel-*kuja*

star-*iltamon*

stream-*arlek*

strength-*puontoneth*

such-*benkat*

summer-*hethtup*

Sun-*iltum*

sword-*nitko*

talent, ability, skill-*chepa*

teamwork-*horgich*

than-*numen*

that-*hro*

their-*mosix*

then, next-*keol*

there-*hefta*

they/them-*masos*

this-*hre*

time-*yewol*

to accomplish, attain-*kigrol*

to add-*bena*

to arrive-*grioudel*

to ask-*puidol*

to augment-*marheno*

to awake-*awanin*

to be able-*skrilay*

to be willing-*velkou*

to be-*huilon*

to bid farewell-*zam*

to bind-*dingra*

to block-*kweltow*

to burn-*zargoth*

to cancel-*xetlan*

to close-*vritui*

to come-*prodo*

to command-*draktoneth*

to connect-*agrakar*

to construct, build-*heklandel*

to control-*chialk*

to counteract-*eknadon*

to cover-*eluonth*

to create (conjure)-*wazak*

to destroy, kill-*hevkel*

to die-*jinakan*

to disappear-*swifnul*

to divide-*lena*

to enchant-*grothar*

to equal-*kuen*

to expand-*buelnos*

to fall-*ektho*

to feel-*lethos*

to fight-*jikona*

to find-*brinol*

to fix-*heranduan*

to follow-*hrikon*

to freeze-*ikanjau*

to gain-*bathue*

to garden, raise children/animals/ plants-*fithwith*

to give-*deknaba*

to go-*quej*

to greet-*nim*

to have-*guenthon*

to heal-*fornijka*

to hit, make contact with-*piktol*

to keep-*mantuona*

to learn-*agravon*

to leave-*delou*

to let-*kuilar*

to lift-*aeronto*

to listen-*horandir*

to live-*jikal*

to look-*eferet*

to lose-*bathnul*

to make-*krelp*

to mean-*velchek*

to merge into one-*oniquon*

to multiply-*kena*

to need-*impertuan*

to open-*pritui*

to protect, shield-*bolkef*

to reduce-*piklir*

to remain-*esklando*

to remember-*mirklir*

to reply, answer-*puides*

to seem-*drijon*

to see-*visyonda*

to share-*neplam*

to smile-*bigren*

to speak-*belforo*

to stand-*uknuf*

to start, begin-*dethuon*

to subtract-*mena*

to summon-*konhekto*

to take-*graglan*

to teach-*landor*

to tell-*fuile*

to thrive, prosper-*glamjan*

to tire, exhaust-*loftana*

to travel-*vemarir*

to use-*grandon*

to want-*lipron*

to win-*molantar*

tree-*suith*

true, authentic, genuine-*trinol*

uncle-*kejla*

variety-*hilups*

water-*lesthra*

way-*yewan*

we-*lami*

whale-*kiga*

what-*kefra*

when-*klepa*

where-*kental*

which-*kodri*

who, that-*kol*

why-*kuar*

wife-*volsek*

wind-*panthuerno*

wolf-*wolshi*

woman, female-*shaba*

woodpecker-*jikavas*

world, nature-*sristik*

you (plural)-*lajas*

you (singular)-*laja*

young-*grendop*

your (plural)-*lajix*

your (singular)-*laj*

0-*ūz*

1-*ăz*

2-*āz*

3-*ĕz*

4-*ēz*

5-*ĭz*

6-*īz*

7-*ŏz*

8-*ōz*

9-*ŭz*

Made in the USA
Charleston, SC
28 February 2012